LOST
FOR
WORDS

AOIFE WALSH

ANDERSEN PRESS

Also by Aoife Walsh

Look After Me
Too Close to Home

First published in 2019 by
Andersen Press Limited
20 Vauxhall Bridge Road
London SW1V 2SA
www.andersenpress.co.uk

2 4 6 8 10 9 7 5 3 1

British Library Cataloguing in Publication Data available.

ISBN 978 1 78344 834 0

This book is printed on FSC accredited paper from responsible sources

Printed and bound in Great Britain by Clays Ltd, Elcograf S.p.A.

For Jeff

1

'Relax,' says Aiza. She can probably hear my heart beating.

'It'll be fine,' says Ruby, peeling the ice pack off my face.

'Well, I'm looking forward to hearing everyone tackle this debate. Dallas!' says Mr Chaplin, beaming. 'Come on up.'

I get up. I think I might be about to faint, or worse, fart. I walk straight into Libby's table, and she shoves it back against me, but I make it to the front, and I turn around.

I still can't believe it. We got through our SATs, we're about to leave primary school in like, six weeks or something, and Mr Chaplin ups and tells us we're going to do public speaking and debate. I mean, it's literally like a nightmare. He hasn't made me do anything difficult since last October and then yesterday out of nowhere he told me I was listed to go first.

My stepmother Gemma told me to pretend I'm just talking to my friends, so I fix on Ruby's eager face at the back, and Aiza who has her head down on her arm. I know she's drawing ninjas, and I know she's not looking at me so as not to freak me out, but every other sarcastic pair of eyes in the class is still fixed right on me. My older brother Sam told me to breathe, so I do. I look down at the damp piece of paper that has my notes written on it, and I say, 'What Makes A Good Brexit?'

Everyone laughs. I said it too loud.

'There is no such thing as a good Brexit,' I say. Defiantly. At least I hope so. Sam, who is clever, said to start with a strong line, then people won't even listen to the rest. I wish my heart would stop thumping in my ears.

'The prime minister can say what she likes,' I say, sounding weak, 'because she didn't even want Brexit, and nearly all the politicians lied on both sides anyway, so I don't know about you, but I don't want to be stuck on a small island with just them. I'd rather take my chances with lots of French and Greek and Polish people, actually.'

I didn't get the line anywhere near right, the way Gemma said I should say it – I can't even remember how that should be now, but nobody's listening anyway. The weird thing is they're all screaming with laughter. My stomach has gone from very hot to very cold. I refocus on my friends. Ruby has her head politely tilted to one side, but Aiza is sitting up and making slashing signs across her throat. I stare at her, feeling dizzy, and wonder how much of my five minutes is left.

'I think we should be trying to be friends with more people,' I stumble on, 'not less. And taking more . . . responsibility.' I gaze at Gilbert Finch, who is howling. He hurls a scrunched-up piece of paper at me. It hits me in the middle of my forehead. Libby whispers something behind her hand to Jada, who cackles. I think that the class in general is tired of giving me a break as well.

I twist round. Mr Chaplin is sitting forward in his chair, with his elbows on his knees and his fingers in his mouth.

'Dallas,' he says, removing them. 'Sorry, Dallas.'

I gaze at him.

'The title of the speech I asked you all to prepare was – actually – "What makes a good breakfast?"'

Afterwards, walking home, Aiza gets halfway through telling me it wasn't that bad, and that it's my own fault for not listening properly, before she starts laughing. I ignore her and pretend to look at my phone. Sometimes when I get it back from the office after school there's a text from my aunt Jessi in Texas, who's the only person who ever texts me besides Aiza and Ruby – but she hasn't sent anything since last night.

Aiza is still laughing. I'm almost glad I'm not going round to her house for once – her dad's taking her to Atomic Pizza even though it's Thursday. Which leaves Ruby and me going off to our own houses. I haven't been home this early in weeks.

Then my almost gladness makes me forget to cross the road in time, and we're suddenly walking past the library – so close that the door slides open and a smell of hot books comes wafting out and I breathe it right into the back of my head before I know what I'm doing.

3

'What's the matter?' asks Ruby.

I will not let this ruin my week. I will not let a perfectly good Thursday, humiliations aside, be made miserable. I'm in charge of my feelings.

Ruby goes her way when we reach the river, and I trudge along the towpath, waiting for the lurch I get every time I come home. It comes when I turn off along our backwater, under the tangled-up ash keys and honeysuckle.

We live in an old boathouse. Its back is built on the bank, but its front sticks out into the river, on two legs, with a big gap in between where the boats used to live. Momma saw it ten years ago when I was a baby and she'd taken Sam and me on a barge holiday. She came from Texas so she thought it was romantic to live in a building two hundred years old, and she wanted somewhere away from streets and roads. I don't know. I used to like it fine, but lately it seems like there are far too many people and at the same time not enough people living in it.

There's the lurch. I think hard instead about what to say when they ask me how my speech went – Sam spent ages telling me Brexity statistics last night – even Gemma, who is always very busy and only sits still when she's making sandwiches or on the computer, kept giving me tips about public speaking because she works at the council.

The door stands open. In summer at this time of day it gets hot and breathless in the house, and our patch of what we call a garden is too full of sun, even if you don't mind

4

being looked at by dog walkers. Lonesome our cat is sprawled on the front step. He blinks at me as I stoop and ruffle the brindle fur by his face, and kick off my sandals.

It's gloomy when you step inside on a bright day – there are only small windows downstairs. I can hardly see anything, but I can hear Sam and Gemma having a row.

'You know what I think about this, Sam.'

'I couldn't give a flying toss what you think.'

'You've been planning which university to go to your whole life . . .'

'What would you know about my whole life? You've only been here three years.'

'Hi,' I say.

Gemma glances sideways from whatever she's pounding in the pestle and mortar. 'How was school?'

'Fine,' I say.

'Good. There's a load of washing on the bed, put it away for me, there's a good girl.'

'I said I'd do that,' says Sam.

'Yes, you did,' says Gemma.

'So you mean I can't be trusted to do what I've said I'll do?'

Gemma sighs. 'I don't mean anything except that I'd like the washing to be put away. This house isn't big enough to have great heaps of sheets lying . . .'

'Here we go,' says Sam. Sam is eighteen and has just finished his A levels which I thought would mean he'd start bossing me around again, but he's still too busy with Billy.

What they argue about at the moment is whether he's going to go on to university. He says he doesn't have time, he's got to look after Billy (and me: ridiculous), and why do we all assume he ought to go to uni when he doesn't even have his A-level results yet. Which is funny because he was predicted to come top in the country or something.

I leave them to it and go over to the sofa, where Billy is watching *They Might Be Giants* on the laptop with his feet in the air. Billy is my little brother, he's autistic and he's four. He's starting school in September. I get the feeling that this doesn't help how anxious everyone is all the time. He doesn't say anything, or glance away from the screen, but when I sit down he shuffles over and climbs on to my lap. I look across at Sam, his head almost scraping the ceiling the way it has done since he was fourteen, and try to imagine what it will be like if he really leaves.

'Isn't that stupid DVD *over* yet?' Violet, my stepsister, asks shrilly from the bottom rung of the ladder.

'Nearly,' I say. 'Were you up in my room?'

'No,' she says, which is ludicrous because there is hardly anything else up the ladder besides my room, which is basically just a bed, and Sam's and Billy's room, which is basically two beds and also smells of boy. I give her a look. 'I wasn't, OK? Mummy! Dallas says I was in her room and I wasn't.'

'Dallas,' Gemma calls, 'she was in the wardrobe. Leave her alone, will you?'

Violet pulls a face at me.

'Why were you in the wardrobe?'

'I have to try on stuff for school.'

'You don't start school for nearly three months.'

'Yeah, like you don't think about it,' she says.

I sigh. 'You're four.'

'So what?'

There isn't any point arguing with Violet, like ever. I hear Gemma telling Sam that she's perfectly capable of taking care of the whole family, and I hear Sam not-quite-saying what we all know he thinks – that Gemma is too busy working and running the house and stuff and looking after Violet to be the perfect stepmother to Billy (and me, I suppose) and that anyway Billy likes Sam best. Then he stamps past and goes up the ladder and a couple of seconds later Steve Earle blasts down from upstairs – crashing chords and sneery voice, singing about being born his papa's son, and wandering eyes, and smoking guns.

I put my arms round Billy. Maybe the best thing about my little brother is that when you're sad, or when he's sad, he'll let you hang on to him for as long as you want. Sometimes he goes to sleep with his nose in my neck.

'Can we watch it again?' he says.

Dinner is pasta. Billy and Violet have bread and butter with it, and when I look sad Gemma sighs and chucks the butter knife towards me, so I have some too.

'Did you tell Dallas about the library?' Sam asks.

Apparently he's stopped sulking, although you never know with Sam – sometimes he pretends to be over things and then bites you in half out of nowhere.

I look at him, and at Gemma, who's pouring apple juice and doesn't answer. 'What about the library?' I ask.

Sam drops more cheese on top of Billy's pasta. 'They're closing it down.'

'I don't like pasta,' says Billy, which if you didn't know him would sound like 'I don't height pasta' – he can't say his ls or cs.

'What?' I say.

'Yes you do,' Sam tells Billy. 'They're closing down the library after all. Going to knock it down and build flats. Isn't there any orange juice?'

'They're not really going to do it, though, right?' I say.

Sam shrugs. 'Apparently.'

'If Billy doesn't eat his pasta can I not eat mine?' asks Violet.

'No,' says Gemma, 'you cannot not eat yours.'

'Billy is going to eat his pasta,' says Sam.

'Are you serious?' They first tried to shut down the library three years ago, because Gracie Gallagher who lives on a boat near us and basically is the only librarian at Queen Street was going to retire, but then she didn't and it was all OK. And then we heard they were thinking about it again last autumn, because people were saying luxury flats were going to be built there instead, but I thought it had all gone away.

'What do you care?' says Sam. 'You haven't been inside it in months.'

There is nobody in the world as good at missing the point as my family. It's true I haven't been in the library. It's also true that I try to shut my eyes or stare in the other direction every time I pass it, which I do at least twice every day. It's not like I don't have reasons, I just don't like to talk about them. For one thing I've been off reading – I mean you never know what a book will do to you. A sentence can sneak up on you and punch you in the neck and start you crying when you thought you were finished with all that and even in books you know, you don't always remember what's coming in time. Most books try and get you at some point, especially old books, like the ones I used to like, and if I carry on like this I'm going to start thinking about *The Railway Children* or something and the whole month will be shot and I'll just have to stay in bed.

'But,' I say. 'I mean, I used to be in there every day.'

'I know,' Sam says.

'Gracie can't keep on going forever,' says Gemma. 'Eat your pasta, Billy.'

'And Billy loves it,' I say. The library. Not the pasta apparently.

'So does Violet,' says Gemma.

'Violet only likes it for the computers,' says Sam.

'At least I don't try and unplug them all the time like Billy,' says Violet.

'When?' I ask. 'When's it shutting down?'

'Late July,' Sam tells me. 'The same day school finishes. Are you drinking that juice?'

'Bloody HELL,' I shout, because they're all so annoying and Billy's just shoved his finger in my ear and what about the library that they're all supposed to care about so much?

'We don't need shouting at the dinner table, thank you, Dallas,' says Gemma.

'Looking for a reason to go into a sulk or something, Dallas?' says Sam.

Billy picks up two handfuls of pasta and throws them at the wall.

'For Christ's sake, Dallas, now look what you've done,' says Sam.

I offer to wash the dishes, but Gemma has the face on which says she'll fight to the death to protect her right to hide in the kitchen with the stereo tonight, so I end up in charge of Billy because Sam is getting ready to go out with his girlfriend Prue.

'Shall we go and see Gracie?' I ask him.

'No,' he says. 'Let's play snakes and ladders.'

'Go and get it then. Do you want to play?' I ask Violet, because she's hanging around.

'No,' she snaps. 'Snakes and ladders is boring.'

'Dallas,' Gemma says. I look up and she's leaning against the counter with soapy water dripping off her rubber gloves.

'If you . . . If you're upset about the library closing – because I know what it used to mean to you – well, maybe you need to start going back in there again. While you still can.'

'No!'

'Don't panic,' she says gently. 'Nobody's going to force you to . . .'

'Good, because no. I can't. I . . .'

'Hey, y'all,' a voice calls. The door is pushed right open and my aunt Jessi, cowboy hat tilted over one eye, bursts over the step holding a guitar case and a bag of duty-free bottles. 'You tellin' me you went and ate without me?'

We weren't expecting her.

Jessi lives in Austin, though she travels all around Texas with her job, nursing. We haven't seen her since last November, although since I got my phone we've been texting a lot. She always did like to surprise us.

She throws herself on my neck so I almost buckle. 'How's my best girl that's suddenly – holy crap – as tall as her old auntie and getting near as pretty?'

'Yeah,' I say, holding on to her tightly. 'Not too bad.'

'Lord God, if you ain't turning into the image of your momma.'

'Gosh you should have let us know, we'd have met you or something,' says Gemma through tight lips.

'What are you doing here?' asks Sam.

Billy whimpers. Jessi is older and thinner and has blonde streaks in her hair but she looks like Momma, if someone

11

had chewed her. And sounds like her too. Billy gets behind Sam, his face crumpling.

'It's just the shock,' Gemma says, sweeping all the cheese off the table with the back of her hand and crashing her chair into place. 'Have you come straight from the airport?'

'Where are you planning to stay?' Sam says.

Jessi ignores Billy being behind Sam's legs and gets right down on the floor to put her hand on his head. 'Billy-o,' she says. 'My hero. Your brother and sister looking after you right?'

'Who is she?' Violet asks loudly.

Jessi reaches up and pats Sam on the behind. 'Don't you fret, Samuel, I got my little tent. You know I'm used to roughing it.'

'Just as well,' Sam mutters.

I'm glad she's brought her tent because it means she can stay as long as she wants, and it's true that we don't have anywhere to put her. My bedroom isn't a room, it's just one side of the loft with a floor that's all bed, and it's the same for Sam and Billy in their side. Gemma and Violet sleep downstairs behind screens.

Before Gemma – when Momma was still married to my dad – Jessi always came to stay during the times when my dad was away being a soldier. So she used to share Momma's bed. Then years later when Gemma and Violet moved in, Jessi started bringing her tent and sleeping in the meadow. Sometimes I'd sleep out too. One night, the summer before last, there was a meteor shower and we had to hold on to each other because it was so incredible, like we were the only people on earth seeing this magic. And we both broke at the same time and went running back to the boathouse to wake everybody before it was too late, especially Momma.

I go over to the meadow behind our house with Jessi and help set up her tent near the biggest willow tree. Then we walk up to the towpath and sit down so she can smoke a cigarette. We look at the sky and the trees on the other bank and listen to the crickets and the river plashing. When she's finished smoking she puts her arm round me and I lean against her. Something in my stomach almost hurts, like being able to unclench your fist after your hands have been really cold – just having her sitting here on the bank beside me, looking at the water.

'What are you thinking about?' she asks me, when the sky is darkening. We talk a little. I tell her about the Brexit/ breakfast cock-up and she laughs her head off and I don't mind. I don't tell her about the library. I just don't feel like going into it.

Last October, everyone around Queen Street and the river was saying that this woman Ophelia Silk who'd just been elected as council leader was going to sell the library to people who would knock it down and build flats on it. And my mother got worked up – she often did get worked up – and started a campaign to save the library. She asked me one afternoon after school if I would come with her and help deliver some leaflets, but I was tired so I said no. I said I had to go to the library and get out a book – I'd just finished *Northern Lights* so I wanted the next one. She said if we didn't do something I wouldn't have a library at all soon and then what would I do – she nagged me all the way there, until I left her and went in – but it wasn't a serious argument.

Because I wouldn't go with her, she went on her bike instead of walking. She got knocked off it and she died. Apparently a lorry driver didn't look when he was turning left.

2

'Dallas!' Gemma screams from the kitchen. 'If you don't come and get your breakfast this second you're going to be late for school AGAIN and I'm going to get another one of those letters.'

Sam mutters something. He's trying to get Billy's T-shirt on but Billy's too busy watching *Bugs Bunny* to put his arms in the right place.

'What was that, Sam?'

'I said—'

'All right, I don't care what you said.' Gemma gives me a shove towards the kitchen. 'Your Weetabix has turned to sludge; we need to start getting you up earlier in the mornings.'

Jessi saunters in wearing a vest and shorts, which would be too short even on me. Though Gemma should be glad she's wearing anything at all – she never does at home. 'Ah,' she says, 'look at you in your uniform. Cute as a button.'

'Thanks,' I say.

'You're up early,' Gemma says.

'Right. I'm still on Texas time.'

'It's half past one in the morning in Texas,' says Sam.

'That's when I come alive, Sammy.'

Sam snorts.

'Ain't it a shame it's a school day. I'd love it if you could take the day off and hang out – do a little shopping maybe . . .'

'No,' says Gemma, before I even get a chance to look at her. She comes in stuffing her purse in her bag. 'Violet, pick up those cards. Billy, get your shorts on please. Time for breakfast and then straight out to nursery.'

Billy doesn't take his eyes off Yosemite Sam.

'You're going to have to wait till this episode's over,' Sam says, dragging Billy's shorts up his legs.

'That's great. They love it at work when I turn up late for my meeting and tell them it's because of *Bugs Bunny*.'

'I'll take him,' Sam says.

'I could stay off,' I say. Usually I wouldn't bother even to ask when it's obviously hopeless, but Jessi expects me to put up a fight. 'SATs are over, we're not doing anything . . .' Not that anyone at home cared about my SATs, which I suppose was a relief. And Sam's A levels – Gemma talked about them a lot, but Sam didn't. He wouldn't even tell her about the exams after he did them, which is not how he was two years ago with his GCSEs.

'No,' Gemma says.

'It's too hot to go to school,' I point out hopefully, stirring my spoon around. I hate soggy Weetabix. I'd much rather pour my own cereal in the morning but I think Gemma thinks that as long as she's making breakfast every day she doesn't have to worry about us.

16

'No,' says Gemma, 'it isn't.'

'Gemma,' says Jessi, 'whyn't you go ahead. I'll feed 'em. Sam'll take the kids to their nursery, I'll see Dallas out.'

Gemma hesitates.

'I won't let her ditch school,' Jessi says. 'Swear to God.'

'Oh all right, fine,' says Gemma, then, 'Thank you. I've got this meeting first thing . . .'

Jessi watches her out, and Sam goes up the ladder to get dressed. Then she whoops under her breath and waves her shopping bag. 'I brought breakfast.'

Breakfast to Jessi is four round tubs of ice cream – Daim bar, pistachio, banana-chocolate and blueberry. She starts digging it out while Violet gawps. She's not used to Jessi.

'Bowls,' Jessi says to me. 'I want a piece of all of these. Call Billy,' she says to Violet.

'He's watching *Bugs Bunny*,' Violet says.

Jessi rolls her eyes and tastes the blueberry. 'He'll stop for ice cream, won't he?'

'Billy doesn't like ice cream,' Violet says.

'What?'

'We think it's probably the cold he doesn't like,' I explain.

'OK,' Jessi says. 'Weird. I can fix that.'

'No you can't,' Violet says. 'Ice cream is always cold.'

'That's what you think,' Jessi says, and puts one of the bowls in the microwave.

There isn't any point saving any. Our freezer is tiny and thick with ice and stuffed full of fish fingers and chips, so we

17

might as well eat it all, Jessi says. When Sam comes through even Billy has finished his bowl of warm cream sludge.

'Classy,' says Sam. 'I suppose you know he'll be sick in about half an hour.'

'Momma used to let Jessi feed us ice cream at stupid times,' I mutter as I clang the bowls under the tap.

'She'd make an almighty fuss first,' he points out, starting on his own bowl and flicking water at me.

Jessi says she needs cigarettes, so she sets off with me towards school. We walk along the river, which is hazy this morning, and the hedgerows and the climbers droop down and stroke our heads. Jessi yawns and pushes them away.

'I suppose it's pretty,' she says, stopping for a second to look at the view, 'but it's just all so little. Makes me homesick.'

'Yeah,' I say, although I love the river. I think it's cool how water can just find the lowest ground and the easiest way to get by, and then it just keeps flowing.

'So how's it going, Dallas?'

'OK,' I say.

'Sam seems real stressed.'

I shrug. They used to get on fine, Sam and Gemma. Now I don't know if any of us get on any more, except Sam and Billy.

'He always was an arguer,' Jessi says. 'He still chivvying you around the way he used to?'

'No,' I say. 'He doesn't have time. Looking after Billy like he does.'

We walk up the stony path to Queen Street. I force myself to look at the library, still shuttered tight against the morning. Nothing happens. I picture it shuttered all day. I picture it not here – an oblong yellow block of flats instead, with big windows so that people living there can look at the river in the evenings from behind glass.

'They're shutting it down,' I say. 'Selling the land. After all.'

Jessi lights her last cigarette. 'That's rough on you. What do you reckon your momma would say?'

I shrug.

'Don't you know?'

'I guess.'

'Of course you do. She'd be like a balloon fixing to pop. Don't you like talking about her?'

'No,' I say, 'I do.'

'Gemma doesn't talk about her much?'

'No,' I say, though she tries sometimes. But I'm not up to it yet, nor Sam either, though he talks about Momma to Billy.

Jessi buys me a pack of Love Hearts from the corner shop. I unwrap them even though I've just brushed my teeth. The top one says FIRST LOVE. I offer it to Jessi.

'I'm sweet enough. You keep it,' she says. 'How about first love? You got any nice boys in your class?'

'No,' I say. 'Ew.'

'They'll be thick as fleas on a farm dog at your next school, you wait. How you getting on with Gemma yourself these days?' She looks down the length of the cigarette she's lighting.

I don't know what to say. I don't even know what's true. We used to be a family before Momma died, and Gemma and Violet were in it too, but now nothing's the same. We're all just muddling through I think. That's what my counsellor called it – she said you've got to muddle through till things come together again, if they ever do. And that seems to be something you have to do on your own, because I have enough trouble just trying to have a normal day. I can't stop and wonder about what kind of day Sam's having, or Gemma. And they can't waste energy on me, either, I mean they have Billy and Violet to look after.

'The house seems to be getting kind of smaller,' she says, echoing what I'm thinking, 'now that you all are grown so much. Lord knows it was never huge.'

'The thing is,' I say, because it's easier to talk about this, 'living on a river sounds like it should be romantic, like you should feel free, you know?'

'Sure.'

'And maybe . . . But we're stuck there in that ridiculous house that's just, like, a shed for boats. We don't even have any boats. And the river is just flowing past. And away. So really it feels much more like we're stuck than it would if we lived in a normal house. Anyway.'

She slings an arm over my shoulder. 'Ain't you used to being listened to these days, Dallas?'

'Momma used to say it was dangerous times when *you* listened,' I tell her.

'What?'

'She said you were a talker, not a listener.'

'That's a dirty lie.'

I giggle.

'I'm a fantastic listener,' she embellishes. 'Folks talk about my listening for hundreds of miles round. From the Gulf Coast to the Panhandle . . .'

'Momma said that if you were listening, that was when you wanted something,' I say.

'Your momma was a goddam cynic.'

Aiza and Ruby are waiting for me at the gate. 'Hey, Dallas!' Aiza hoots. 'What did you have for Brexit?'

I roll my eyes.

'Come on, that was one of my best.'

At school we head to the office to hand our phones in to Ms Wilson. 'You got a phone then finally, Dallas?' says Libby, knocking into me from behind. 'It only took you till the last term of Year 6.'

'Yep,' I say. I've had it three months, but whatever. Ms Wilson is watching us. I somehow get the feeling she doesn't like Libby much, but then I expect everybody not to like Libby and yet some people do.

'Have you figured out how to send a text message yet? Have you got anyone to send one to anyway?' She leans over me to make sure her phone is on top of the heap.

'Oh shut up, Libby,' says Aiza, barging in and slinging her phone into the drawer, right on top of Libby's. 'Some people have got better things to think about than getting a new phone every term.'

'Is that why yours is three years old then, Aiza?'

'At least my hairstyle isn't.'

'That's enough, girls,' says Ms Wilson. 'Libby, I hope you've turned your phone off. Last week I was treated to your snooze tone every half hour.'

'Ms Wilson's all right,' Aiza says as we walk towards our classroom. Ruby is waiting for us halfway along the corridor. Libby and Jada jostle her as they barge past, but she just shakes them off.

'Yeah,' I say. I just wish I didn't feel like all the staff are watching me. Maybe Aiza's right, maybe it'll be a relief to be at secondary school where I'm not the kid with the dead mum. I put my arm through Ruby's. Ruby gets watched too because sometimes her mother gets ill or whatever and can't look after her. But Ruby doesn't think about herself the way I think of her. Maybe she likes being in charge and doing the food shopping and things, even if it means she has to wear the same T-shirt a few days in a row.

Libby pushes past as I go to hang up my bag. 'I was

meaning to ask you, Dallas,' she flings over her shoulder. 'What did you have for Brexit today?'

'Pathetic,' Aiza shouts after her. 'Spend all night thinking that one up, did you?'

It's definitely over – the everyone leaving me alone thing.

'How was the pizza?' Ruby asks wistfully as we hang up our bags. Ruby loves food.

'All right,' Aiza says.

'Just all right?'

She frowns. 'Dad was weird. Kept talking about dating.'

I'm shocked. 'You mean, going on dates?'

'Yes. Not me, Dallas, you div, him. And I don't get it because I've always known he's gone on dates. I mean, why does he suddenly want to talk about it? Usually he just says he's working late, and then puts on a flash shirt and loads of aftershave.'

Aiza doesn't have a mum, she left when Aiza was a baby and I don't think she remembers her at all. Her dad's nice though.

'I love Atomic Pizza,' says Ruby. We all went there for Aiza's eighth birthday.

'Not on a Thursday, though,' I say, kicking my chair so it faces the right direction. For the first time ever we're allowed to sit together, now that SATs are over. 'No wonder it was weird. Everyone knows Friday is pizza night.'

'You're so conventional, Dallas,' says Aiza, taking a Love Heart from the packet I've passed her under the table.

23

I wonder. When Sam was thirteen and started getting really embarrassed by us – as in not ever inviting his friends round, not like when he just used to hide me and Momma behind doors – Momma said that he was getting conventional. She also said he'd grow out of it. For his fourteenth birthday we made him a sign, like a bumper sticker, which was purple and blue and silver and said 'Keep Sam Weird'. It was a copy of the signs we'd seen in Austin last time we were there. Austin is the place in Texas where all the hippies and the vegans and people like that live, and naked men riding horses. You see signs everywhere that say 'Keep Austin Weird'. Sam didn't even laugh when he saw it, but he kept it. It's stuck on his door now.

Momma never felt the need to make a sign like that for me. Maybe if I'd got to thirteen she might have done.

'They're closing the library,' I say.

'What library?' Aiza asks, opening her book.

'Are they?' Ruby says, struggling with the Love Hearts. 'The one near the river?'

Aiza smooths down her page, picks up her pen, glances up at me. 'So what?'

'So,' I say. 'I don't think I want them to.'

'Then stop them,' Ruby says brightly.

'How's she going to do that?'

Ruby shrugs. 'People stop people doing stuff all the time. Just tell them.'

'You never even go in there any more, do you?' Aiza asks, watching me.

'No,' I admit. I open my own book and look at the task written on the board. 'I thought I might, though. Maybe tomorrow.'

'Oh look, Dallas.' Ruby is squinting at her Love Heart. 'MIR – MIRACLES – HAPPEN. MIRACLES HAPPEN. You see?' She beams.

'Nice reading,' Libby mocks from behind us.

'Miracles happen,' Ruby says to her.

'Yeah, so get stuffed,' says Aiza.

I make a mental note not to bring any more wordy sweets into school.

Lunch is fish and chips, but they're always cold, and the guy who serves on a Friday thinks it's hilarious to hum the theme tune to some old TV programme called *Dallas* whenever he sees me. After seven years I've run out of ways to smile and nod so he can see I'm not offended. I can hear him laughing the whole time I'm walking with my tray to the far end of the hall. 'I hate my name,' I mutter.

'Why?' Aiza is halfway through her lunch already, even though she was only two ahead of me in the queue. She does everything fast.

'Er, because I'm not a horse-riding gun-slinging lasso-swinging cowboy who cuts the heads off cactuses for drinking water. I'm eleven and I'm a girl. In Oxford. In England.'

'The plural of cactus,' says Aiza, 'is cacti.'

'It's also cactuses. Look it up in the dictionary.'

'You look it up in the dictionary.'

'My nan's got a cactus,' says Ruby. Ruby eats slowly, one chip at a time. 'On her windowsill. Above the kitchen sink.'

'And you're telling us that why?' Aiza licks the foil top of her yoghurt pot and flicks it across the table at Gilbert Finch.

'I don't think you'd get much water out of it though,' Ruby says. 'It's only the size of the soap dish.'

'Easier just to turn on the tap in the sink then, eh, Rubes?' Aiza rolls her eyes. 'Anyway, I think it's cool. It means something – a place. Aiza just means "noble", that's well boring. I mean all names mean that.'

'Ruby doesn't,' says Ruby, moving on to her fish.

'No, true, that's much better. A precious jewel! A blood-red stone! The things Dorothy had on her shoes!' Aiza shouts. 'And Ruby Cox is a brilliant name. Like Dallas Kelly. It's cool to sound like a cowboy.'

I mutter.

'It is! Oh look.' She grabs my arm. 'Get ready.'

Libby and Jada and Sophie are sitting at the next table over. We watch as Libby opens up her Cath Kidston lunchbox again and brings out her doughnut. Her special, pink-candy-stripe-wrapped London doughnut.

Jada nudges her. She glances up and sees us looking. 'Lemon meringue this week,' she calls down the table to us.

I mean, I don't know who she thinks she is. Just because

her mum works in London and brings her a posh doughnut for Fridays. I would have stopped talking about it years ago and not given her the satisfaction, but Aiza enjoys mocking her too much, and Ruby – she just can't not look.

'Mmm,' Libby calls. 'Delicious.' She dabs her mouth with a napkin. 'If only they did them ten in a bag for a quid from Lidl, eh, Ruby?'

'Cow,' Aiza says.

3

I used to stay in bed reading on Saturday mornings. Billy and Violet always get up at the crack of dawn and start scrapping – well, Violet scraps and Billy just does whatever he wants and occasionally smacks her in the face. Now that I don't read much I usually get up too. And after I've sat glazed on the sofa in front of cartoons, while Gemma and Violet go out to buy food for the week, Gemma needs me to help put the food away and do all the hoovering and stuff.

'I do not understand your clothes habits, Dallas,' she says, loading the washing machine. 'Your laundry is as unpredictable as the spring tide. Every morning you swear to me you've put your dirty stuff in the washbin, but I've gone all week without seeing a single pair of your pants, and here is an entire wash made up your clothes.'

To be honest it's a mystery to me as well.

'What are you doing today?'

'I'm going round to Aiza's after lunch,' I say.

'Surprise surprise. What do you do there all the time?'

'Watch *Columbo*.'

She grins. Everyone thinks it's hilarious that we like

watching this detective programme that was made about fifty years ago or something, but it's good. 'All right, but I need you to do something for me on the way.'

'What?'

'Drop these off at the library.' She taps a big pile of picture books, all casual. My heart thumps.

'Why do I have to do it?'

'Because you're the one walking past it,' Sam snaps from the floor by our ancient freezer, where he's trying to cram in a bag of chips.

'Therapy,' Gemma says.

'My therapist said not to force anything.'

'Your therapist didn't know it was closing down.'

'Well hell,' says Jessi's voice, 'I was expecting to find you all still tucked up in bed and here you all are jumping like hot grease on a skillet.'

Violet stands up with her hands on her hips. 'It's nearly lunchtime. I've been up for more than four hours.'

'Ain't you great?'

'Jessi,' says Gemma, gathering up all the clean washing in a big heap. 'How are you after the night in the tent?'

'If I felt any finer I'd suspect a set-up,' Jessi says, taking an apple from the fruit bowl and winking at me.

'I've forgotten, Billy,' Sam says, getting up to start making lunch. He says it every week. 'Is it ham and cheese sandwiches you like, or cheese and ham?'

'Ham and CHEESE!' Billy cries.

'It's the same thing,' says Violet, rolling her eyes.

I try to go into the library. I plunge up the steps towards the door, past where I left her that evening, and almost bash my face on the glass – it seems the motion-sensor thing isn't working any more. But there's the same old *whuff* as I push the door open instead, and the smell of books and warm carpet hits me in the face. The only thing I see clearly is the old red D cushion I always used to sit on – some little kid is lying on his stomach on it now, reading. I was sitting on that cushion with *The Subtle Knife* when Sam came in to tell me we had to go to the hospital.

The pile of books tips in my hands. I nearly just lob them on to the floor for someone else to find, but as Gemma would say, I was brought up better than that.

I take them with me instead, as I tiptoe out and walk away.

'What are those?' asks Aiza, standing back to let me in.

'Library books to return,' I say airily.

Ruby looks up from the pink sofa, where she's tucked in a corner eating Rolos. 'Are you going to stop them shutting it?'

'No,' I say, 'because it turns out I can't even go inside. I hope there's more chocolate because I need some.'

'Don't question my hostessing,' says Aiza, dumping a huge box of Milk Tray on the table.

* * *

'So,' Aiza starts after we've watched an episode of *Columbo* – the one with the politician, not one of my favourites. Aiza got us into *Columbo* last year after she had chickenpox, the same week their broadband connection broke so she had to watch TV all day.

'I didn't understand a word of that,' Ruby says, chewing thoughtfully on a salted caramel charm.

'It didn't make much sense,' I agree. 'I mean that whole bit with the fake gunshots, that was stupid.' I get up to put on *Lemonade*. Beyoncé is the only music we all like.

'I just don't think Columbo would do that kind of thing,' Ruby says. 'Pass me the crisps?'

'Girls,' Aiza says in a firm voice, 'you're not listening to me.'

We turn towards her, which makes Ruby knock the bag out of my hand, and Wotsits go everywhere.

'I think we need to talk,' she carries on loudly.

I tap Ruby's arm to stop her putting fallen Wotsits back in the bag. 'That's disgusting, they'll fester. At least eat them now.'

'All right.' She crams a handful in. 'Isn't it funny how they turn everything orange. Your dad won't mind will he, Aiza?'

'Look, I'm trying to have a meaningful conversation.'

I look up at her, but I carry on picking up Wotsits by feel. I like her white carpet.

'I want to know why you can't go into the library, Dallas.'

'What?' I say, looking down again.

'We know how much you used to be in there, it was like your living room. I mean, you used to make us go in there.'

'Not me,' says Ruby. 'I don't like libraries. God, I'm full of chocolate.'

'Ruby, stop making it so easy for Dallas to avoid answering! Dallas. Talk to us.'

'No,' I say. 'I mean, there's nothing to talk about. I used to go in there a lot. I don't any more. So what?'

'It's to do with your mum, isn't it?'

'Yeah,' I say. I sound angry and I mean to go on and answer fuller but I can't, and anyway, that's the answer.

'Well,' Aiza says. 'OK then.'

'Yeah.'

'But don't you think you should . . .'

'Why have you got such a massive box of these anyway?' Ruby asks, groaning as she selects another chocolate.

Aiza scowls. 'I don't know why he even bought them. He came in with them last night, and I said were they for me and he said no, and then this morning he was muttering about how could he buy Milk Tray for such a classy bird and did he think he was going on a date with a barmaid from *Coronation Street*. When he left he said he was going to Hotel Chocolat for some boozy truffles like a lady deserves.'

I laugh, which is a relief because I don't want to get upset, not here.

'So is that where he is right now?' Ruby asks, picking out a strawberry temptation. 'With a lady?'

Aiza snorts. 'At the cinema. He asked me if I wanted to go. Can you imagine?'

'I like the cinema,' Ruby says. She looks at the clock. 'I've got to go home.'

'Yeah,' I say with a sigh. 'Me too.'

'I don't want to.'

'Me neither.'

Ruby doesn't comment when I walk straight past the library with my armful of picture books. 'What are you doing tomorrow?' she asks instead.

'Hanging out with Jessi, probably. What about you? Aren't you going to your nan's?'

She shrugs. 'Mum and her had another fight, so probably not.'

'Everyone's fighting,' I say.

'Yeah. It's too hot, that's what I think.'

It is hot. In the evening it's so still that I hear Sam talking to Gracie on the towpath. I'm sitting on our tiny bridge over our little weir, trying to get Lonesome to talk to me, but he keeps edging away.

'And I know how you all are with your pride but there isn't any shame in asking for help or sympathy is there, and what do you call that face, young Samuel?'

Sam sighs. 'Gracie, that's just how I look.'

'Resting crank face,' I say to Lonesome.

There's a screech. 'Is that my little Dallas? Come here where I can see you, pet.'

I get up and wander through the grass towards the towpath. 'Hi.'

'Hi, is it, when I haven't laid eyes on you in must be three weeks till this morning. And then you just stood on the threshold for half a second and ran off.' Gracie has lived in the nearest boat to us for years and years. 'I'm telling you both there's no power in it, all this stiff upper lip. You haven't even a drop of English blood the either of you. Do you talk to Gemma now?'

I sigh. It's not that I've got loads of stuff I want to talk about or I want to have millions of heart to hearts, but it is very hard to talk when Gemma always has so much work to do in the evenings and any time I do open my mouth one of the kids squawks and she has to run out of the room to see what's wrong with them, and all Sam does is strop around looking moody even though he's finished his exams and he's supposed to be relaxed.

Sam gives me side-eye. 'Yes,' he says.

'Well I hope so, but she's almost as bad as the pair of you. Every time I see her it's work or nursery or the special needs people, never a thought of letting the grief out.'

'Mmm,' I say.

'You're dead right of course, I was talking to Father Joseph about you all and didn't he say the same thing as you, that everybody has to get through it their own way. And if you need to stay out of the library for a while then that's understandable, with all the memories.'

'Er,' I say.

'You're right, and maybe it's just as well to cut loose since the place is closing.' She puffs and sighs.

'Is it definitely?' I ask.

'It is, love. I was hoping they'd find a way to keep it going but they won't. I rang them up and said could I withdraw my resignation again but they said not this time, they can't afford me, imagine it.'

'But what about the campaign, it might work mightn't it?'

'What campaign? There's no campaign, darling, that died with your mother, God rest her. There aren't many round here who'd get up and do something like her.' She gazes at me. 'So many things changing. It always used to be Sam was off somewhere and now he's always here and I never seem to see you except flying past on a bicycle. What is it you do with yourself these days, Dallas?'

Sam snorts.

'Not much,' I say. 'I go round my friend Aiza's quite a lot.'

'Is that the little Muslim?'

We wince.

'And isn't it just her and her father living in that house? Mmm. Well now, if it was up to me I'd be wanting to know a man like that pretty well before I was letting you go off there all hours . . .'

'I think it's time we said goodnight, Gracie, you lovable old racist,' Sam says.

'What? Now it isn't anything at all about them being Muslims or what have you, it's only that I'm suspicious of men with no women to keep any eye on them. How would you be calling me a racist against Muslims when you know how I feel about Malala?' Momma gave her a copy of *I Am Malala* when it first came out. I've seen where she keeps it, next to her bed with her rosary beads.

After Gracie's gone back to her boat, I sit back down on the bridge. I always used to like sitting here, looking at the sky and the different colours it goes, and the birds, and primroses or red bracken or whatever was going on. Now I just look at the water flowing past, and think about the library, and nobody bothering to try to save it.

Lonesome stands up and walks over to Sam. He rubs his head down Sam's cheek, then prowls away, completely ignoring me and the kissing noises I'm making. I watch him skulk along the bank towards the boathouse. 'Why doesn't he love me?'

'Because you bullied him when you were little,' Sam says. 'He's older than you, he remembers the peace before you came.'

Even the cat doesn't like me best

I'm WhatsApping Ruby and Aiza. It's only after I send it that I think it sounds a bit tragic, not like I'm joking, which I was.

Ruby answers straight away.

Its only me and mum in our house and we still dont like each other best

I'm thinking what to say to that when Aiza replies.

Do you want a prize you pair of sadsacks

4

There's beef for dinner on Sunday.

'Real English,' says Jessi. 'Wild. So, Dallas, let's hear some ideas about how to stop this thing.'

'What thing?' Sam asks.

'The library closing,' I explain. He snorts.

I talked to Jessi about it today, in the meadow. But I'm embarrassed in front of Gemma and Sam, and anyway I don't have any ideas, so Jessi talks about protests she's been on, specially with Momma when they were young. Sam tries to stuff carrot into Billy's mouth, but Billy keeps batting his hands away.

'So you try some marches and demonstrations. On the library steps . . .'

'All two of them?' Sam says. 'Billy, come on. Just a mouthful.'

'I ate mine,' Violet says.

'Maybe at the town hall, make some noise, make sure the press is there. Then when that fails . . .'

'If it's going to fail, why bother?' Sam asks.

'First of all, because there's a *process*,' Jessi tells him. 'Secondly, I meant *if* it fails. Then you can tailor it a little bit more. I mean, it's a library. You could try occupying the building. If it goes down to the wire.'

Billy finishes his fifth Yorkshire pudding. Sam sticks a spoon in his carrot and sighs.

'Come on,' says Gemma. 'Let's have it. Why hold back?'

'Look,' Sam says, 'I just worry about Billy.'

We all look at Billy, who's pinching another Yorkshire off my plate.

'What's wrong with Billy? He's OK.'

'Yes,' Sam says, 'but he's not going to eat the carrot or the swede or even the potatoes because he never does, you know that, and frankly I'm concerned about the state of his bowels.'

'That is frank,' says Jessi.

'Sam,' Gemma says, 'this is exactly what I'm talking about. You're eighteen, you're never going to be eighteen again, you should be out living and reading great books that expand your mind and travelling and – you should not be worrying about your brother's bowels.'

'Someone's got to,' says Sam. 'And while I'm at it, stop filling Dallas's head with ideas about the library. When you both know it's going to shut down in July, whatever you get her to do.'

I wash up later on, after Sam's gone to see Prue. He'll probably stay with her tonight, he does when he looks that tired. I try to listen to Miranda Lambert on the stereo and not to Gemma and Jessi, who are having a polite argument about Sam. And everything. At least it's polite, which is more than I can say for the five minutes after Gemma found out about the ice cream for breakfast on Friday.

'I can see his point,' Jessi says. 'He's bound to see you got your hands full. I mean, with four kids and a job . . .'

'I manage,' says Gemma. She sounds snarky. I can tell she's dying for Jessi to leave so she can flip open her computer and get on with her work.

'Of course, I know Dallas is at her friend's place a lot.' They both look at me. Gemma's eyes are like diamonds. 'That must worry you, Gemma.'

'Not really,' Gemma says. 'Her therapist said it would take time to adjust and for things to settle down. It's only been eight months.'

'Eight months is a long time when you're eleven years old,' says Jessi.

Aiza's house is more comfortable than home, I admit it to myself. Last November I couldn't stand to be here – Billy was always screaming and everywhere there was this hole, upstairs and downstairs, where she should have been. I used to roam around the back of the bridge road in the mist and smell people's garden bonfires, till I started going to Aiza's. Home isn't that bad any more. It's just different.

'I'm going to give the kids a shower,' Gemma says.

'Did you go in the library yet?' Aiza asks me next day.

'I hate the library,' I say. 'And I hate books.'

'Right then,' she says. 'Do you want to come round tonight? My dad's out again.'

'I can't.'

'Rabia's making that curry you like,' she wheedles. Rabia is her childminder.

'I can't. Gemma told me to come straight home.' I think Jessi must have got to her.

Aiza shrugs. 'Just you and me then, Rubes.'

'I can't either,' Ruby says. 'I'm staying with my nan again.'

I do go straight home after school and I shouldn't have bothered because Violet's pitching a huge hissy fit and Billy's all white and floppy and just while Gemma's in a flurry getting dinner on the table he's sick on the bed – not his bed but Momma's, where Gemma sleeps by herself now. Sam's gone to the cinema with Prue so there isn't anyone to help Gemma change the duvet – I'm cleaning Billy up. Then after dinner Lonesome unfortunately goes and does a poo on the fresh duvet cover. Lonesome is old now and sometimes he disgraces himself.

I hear a lot of door slamming going on, and I look out of my bedroom window and see Gemma stalking away towards the towpath with a bin bag full of washing hoiked up on her shoulder.

I make sure Billy's still asleep, and then I finish the dishes that Gemma's left half done, since I'm pretty sure she's not in the mood, and then I peep behind her curtains just to check the bed is clean. Momma's favourite duvet cover is on the bed – it's this pretty burnt orange, like a flower I don't know the name of. I haven't seen it in months. I go in just to see if it still smells of Momma, and it does, and it's all smoothed out – Gemma's one of the people who always does things extra carefully when she's angry. I just lie down for a minute. I'm not feeling brilliant, and I wonder if I'm getting what Billy's got, only with me it's mostly a weird backache that's been there on and off all day. Because I'm always fiddling with stuff, I start sliding one of the drawers of the bedside table in and out. I look at the smears of pale green paint on the ceiling – Momma painted the whole place and it was the first time she'd done that so she was proud, but the ceiling did get a bit smudgy. I always used to count them when I was ill and Momma put me in her bed, or when I got in with her on a Saturday morning, and next thing the curtains swing open and Gemma starts yelling – it makes me feel as if she's chucking stones at me. Then she calms down and goes all despairing and starts rubbing her eyes behind her glasses and that's worse.

'I just need a little – just a tiny bit – of my own space,' she says. 'Moving into this ludicrous house – I know I should be used to it by now, I've been here nearly three years, but – everything's just so hard, Dallas, and I know it is on you too, and I shouldn't have lost my temper but sometimes it feels like I don't have any space at all. Can you understand that, sweetheart?'

I mean, of course I can. I was just seeing if the duvet smelled like Momma still, and obviously I should explain that, but I can't, partly because I can't say things like that at any time and partly because if I try to then I will have to stop concentrating on not crying. And unfortunately right then Sam walks in the front door and distracts me and I snuffle and that's it, tears are definitely falling, which is pathetic.

'Why is Dallas crying?' he says, suddenly beside me. And it's nice to have him standing by me and getting angry because of me, not at me, but also I don't like shouting.

Gemma's still kneading her eyes and talking in this tired voice, explaining what just happened, but Sam seems not to be in an understanding mood either.

'Look,' he says, 'I go out for the afternoon because you tell me everything's going to be fine and I come back and find Billy's been puking up everywhere and meanwhile here you are, taking it out on my motherless sister.'

'Let's not get melodramatic, Sam,' Gemma says. 'Dallas and I have had a chat, that's all, about respecting each other's space, which I know is hard in this house, and trying to make things easier for each other. It's not a big deal.'

'Dallas is eleven,' Sam says. 'She hasn't done anything naughty, she was lying on her mother's bed, because it is her mother's bed, which nobody has ever told her not to do before.'

Gemma looks at him, and her chin trembles.

'Look,' she says, 'we can talk about it later, OK.'

'What's happening?' Suddenly Jessi is behind the curtains as well and there's hardly any floor to stand on, especially since I'm afraid to touch the bed. 'Who made little Dallas cry?'

'I'm not crying,' I say, wiping my chin.

'What's going on?'

'*Nothing*,' says Gemma, and she lifts the nearest curtain up and tugs it round so suddenly Sam and Jessi and I are on the outside of it.

Jessi puts her arm round me. 'You OK?'

'She's fine,' Sam snaps.

'You come on with me, sugar,' Jessi says.

'Leave her alone,' Sam says. 'God, why can't you ever leave anybody alone?'

Jessi stares at him, her arm still over my shoulders. 'Maybe because I'm not half-Brit.'

'Oh shut up,' Sam says. 'Shut up about Texas. As if it's God's own country. My mother hated Texas – she came here to get away from it. From you too, probably.'

'Stop it,' I say, but my voice slides all over the place. I twist away from Jessi, out from between them, and run off, meaning to go to the meadow, only something's happened to my backache, so I go to the bathroom first. Locking the door.

The light in our bathroom isn't strong but I can see the stain in my knickers. And I sit there wondering what to do.

Obviously in theory I know about periods. Momma

wasn't the kind of mother who left you unprepared. And yet I am unprepared, because I don't know who to tell, and I'm pretty sure that you're meant to tell somebody.

I wasn't supposed to start yet. Momma was almost thirteen. I'm not even almost twelve. Maybe it's because I'm squarer than she was. Maybe if I don't eat anything for a few days this will go away. No, that's not a good idea. And it will go away in a few days anyway, that's something to cling on to. A month is a long time. This isn't right, sitting here talking to myself. I should tell somebody.

Probably the obvious thing is to go and tell Jessi. But she'd make a big deal out of it, and I can't bear it, and after her arguing with Sam and Gemma it would be like saying I was on her side against them. But I can't tell Gemma either because then Jessi would be hurt, and anyway . . . anyway this feels like one of those things about us that Gemma never signed up for. That makes me think about how she got stuck with us.

Or I could tell Sam. I get the giggles, picturing it.

Oh well. When it comes down to it it's embarrassing anyway for me to talk out loud to anybody about stuff that's happening with my vagina. I pull out my phone. This is what phones are for.

So guess what. I consider waiting for them to guess, but what if they're not checking their messages right at this second. I can't hang around in the bathroom forever. *My period started.*

It only takes about twenty seconds before it beeps. That's quicker than it would've been if I'd gone to find Jessi or Gemma. And kudos to my friends because I don't know what I would have said if one of them sent me that text. Probably OMG.

OMG

Oh. But then:

Good grief girl this is what happens when you don't come to my house after school your childhood breaks

Thanks Aiza I reply.

When asks Ruby.

Just now. To give them an idea of how just now, I add *Im still in the bathroom.*

Looking at your pants right Aiza comes back. *That's what I did I was in there for about 2 hours*

Wait, what? *I didnt even know youd started you mystery woman*

Thought you were pretty special there for a minute didn't you

Your both weird says Ruby. *I dont know why Im friends with you*

Seriously tho Dallas did you tell your stepmother or aunty or whatever

Pause. *No*

Yeah I can see that writes Aiza. *I had to tell my dad which was weird*

I sit and look at the phone.

He was all right tho once we both stopped blushing

Stop talking for a sec A taps Ruby. *D do you need anything*

I swallow.

Just wanted to tell someone

Gemma's stuff is here, she's got a whole drawerful of sanitary towels, but I know I'll have to get my own or she's bound to notice. Aiza talks me through where in the shop to go, and I nick one of Gemma's for now (*It's not like you're going to be gushing blood the first time*) and plan to nip into town tomorrow after school to get some of my own. *Nothing with wings, they don't work* Aiza advises me, and *Oh you don't want to worry about tampons yet. Save some excitement for when you turn 12*

Gemma's pegging out the washing when I finally come out. The tumble dryer at the laundrette must be bust again. 'I'm sorry, Dallas,' she says. 'Do you want to come in and help me make the dinner?' But then her phone rings, and I'm glad. Really I know she'd rather be on her own. And I want to be on my own too. I'm still all jingled up, and I feel different. Like something big has happened and I need to get away.

I walk through the meadow, over to the biggest willow where Jessi's parked her little green tent. She gets up off the grass when she sees me. It's one of those pearl-blue evenings when you can see the rays of the sun all around. It shouldn't be possible to be in the middle of them and not feel happy.

'You want to talk?'

'No,' I say.

She's rolling a cigarette as we walk, and watching me at the same time. Talk about multi-tasking.

'Whyn't you go off by yourself for a while then.'

'I'm not supposed to be out late on my own.'

'So what?'

I walk right through the meadow and through the nature reserve, getting used to my knickers feeling weird, getting used to being here again. I haven't come this way in months, not since just after Momma died. Everything has got so different, but here it's still the same – quiet and smelling of grass and water. The wildflowers are paler than they would have been a month ago. The embankment isn't as high as it used to be, or I suppose it probably is only my legs are longer.

I walk back by the road. Past the library. It ought to be shut by now, of course it ought, it's meant to shut at six, but Gracie never has the heart to kick anyone out. A tired-looking woman with a pushchair and a little kid is leaving. She's got a big pile of books shoved in under the buggy. A memory hits me, clear as daylight when you pull the curtain in the morning – sitting on the bench there outside because I got a nosebleed pulling a book off a high shelf on to my face. I must have been about Billy's age. There was blood everywhere, all over me down to my socks, and all over Momma too, and she was holding the top of my nose and stroking back my hair and telling me about how noses are so full of blood just so they can heal quickly. I was afraid somebody else would get our books, but she told me it was safe to wait till I stopped squelching gore, that books will always wait, that's why they're so good, and that libraries are the safest, gentlest places in the world.

Sam once said he was bored going to the library, and Momma said to zip his face, that libraries are the most exciting, heart-pumping places in the world.

What I liked best about it, apart from the books, was the way nobody bothered me there. You could sit still and nobody tried to get in your head. And I don't know if it could ever be the same, now. But I'm beginning to realise that *ever* is a long time.

The worst time wasn't after she died. I saw how other people were grieving, and I knew that I wasn't, yet, that I was just waiting. I knew it was coming. I felt like a piñata, hanging from a tree by a cord, and a bunch of people were whacking at me with sticks to make me burst, and I knew once a hole got in me then everything that was normal in my life would fall out. And then I started thinking that maybe I was pinned up too high and they weren't going to reach me with their sticks after all.

Then, after the funeral, I realised I had it wrong. I wasn't a piñata full of stuff in a tree, I was a hollow piñata floating in a sea and the water was gradually soaking through me till I was just pink paper mush and I went under.

That was the worst time.

*   *   *

49

'We have to save the library,' I say the moment I get inside, and Gemma doesn't even shush me, even though Violet must have been tucked up behind her screen for hours. And she doesn't ask me where I've been either.

'We may not be able to,' she says.

'We definitely won't be able to,' says Sam.

'Well,' I say. 'All the same, we have to.'

5

I think about it all day at school, which is weird at the moment. Ever since SATs finished, it's like Mr Chaplin is afraid to make us do any work, so all we're doing is 'fun' stuff and things like the 'debating' about meals which thankfully is over now. Ruby and Aiza notice that I'm distracted. While I'm trying to stick a cardboard robot's arms on, Aiza's own robot bounces off my head.

'Ow!'

'Why are you being all silent, Dallas? What's on your mind? Oh, shut up, it's made out of a Rice Krispies box, it didn't hurt you.'

'It's also got about a kilo of dried glue on it,' I say, rubbing my head. 'I'm just trying to get mine fixed.'

'Why? What for? And you might want to stop sticking a leg in the armhole.'

'Oh,' I say.

'She wants to know what you're thinking about,' Ruby advises me, picking Aiza's robot up.

'Just the library.'

'What about it?'

'Stopping it shut down?' Ruby asks.

I didn't expect them to be interested. I practically grew up in Queen Street library because our house is so small it was like an extra room with a lot of bookshelves. By the time Sam was getting ready for his GCSEs Gracie used to let him stay on to study long after closing time; but that's just us. Ruby's barely ever been in there, and whenever Aiza wants a book she can buy it on her dad's Amazon Prime account and have it the next day. Three walls of her bedroom have shelves on them.

But they listen. They seem, well, keen. None of us can think of much that's useful yet, but I can feel my engine cranking up.

'What's this about the library?' Mr Chaplin has crept up behind us.

'It's closing,' Ruby tells him, 'but Dallas is going to save it.'

'Are you, Dallas?'

Yeah, Dallas, are you? All three of them are looking at me. I suppose it's tempting to laugh and say, probably not, how can I, I'm eleven, and relax and think about lunch instead. The price for that is the library though.

'Yeah,' I say.

Mr Chaplin hitches up his trousers and perches on the side of our table. 'That's really interesting. You know what, you should do an assembly on it. The Head is always looking to get you kids involved in assembly. I bet you could get some real support that way.'

'All right, sir,' says Aiza, turning her back squarely on him to get him to stop engaging with us, 'Dallas will give that some thought.'

'Do,' he says to me, unhitching and wandering off.

'You could,' Ruby says. 'I expect lots of kids here go to the library.'

'Hmm,' says Aiza. 'It would still just be a bunch of children though. They'd either ignore us or call us a mob and fire tear gas at us.'

'What is tear gas?' Ruby asks.

'I don't know. Not the point. You need to dig up some adults, Dallas.'

'Yeah.'

'Dallas.'

'What?'

'You know you're going to have to go in there, right?'

Later when we're walking back, Ruby tells me she's only nipping home to get a bag of stuff because she's still staying with her nan. 'So I hope Paul won't be in.'

'Who's Paul?'

'Mum's boyfriend,' she says patiently, like she's never told me about him before which, now I think of it, she has. But I didn't realise he was still around.

'You don't like him?'

She shrugs. 'He's OK. But it's weird when he's there and Mum's not, and she's got this job now, in that new pub.'

'What new pub?'

'That one on Lantern Street.'

'That's not new.'

'No, but it's got a new name. It's called the Lusty Gardener now.'

'That's ridiculous.'

'They've got a fancy new kitchen. Anyway so she's not at home as much.'

'Is that why you're staying at your nan's?'

'Yeah.' She kicks a pebble into the river. 'She doesn't think Mum should leave me on my own.'

The idea of being at home on my own is weird, there's never no one in our house, but if there was it would be much more lonely than at Ruby's. She lives in a block of flats, so there are always people next door, and above, and below. 'What do you think?'

She shrugs. 'I wish they wouldn't argue about it. Look, there are your brothers.'

I was thinking about Ruby, I hadn't even noticed that we'd turned on to Queen Street, let alone that Sam was leaning against the wall outside the library breaking bits off a banana for Billy. I walk up to them slowly.

'All right,' he greets me.

'Do you just happen to be here?'

'Don't be a div. We're waiting for you.'

'What for?'

He points down at a bag by his feet. 'To return these.' It's the bag of picture books.

It's easier, I guess, with Sam behind me and Billy swinging from my hand.

'Come on, Dallas.'

'All right, all right. I'm a bit scared, Billy.'

'But it's not scary.'

And Ruby there too, behind me, holding my school bag for me as I put my first foot on the first step, and then my second on the second. There are only a few people inside, I can see that from the doorway; the Tuesday Toddler singalong is well over. Gracie is kneeling down in the picture-book section, picking them all up off the floor. Roger's helping her, but his hands are so shaky he can't fit them back in their compartments. Roger is this homeless man that we all know because he spends a lot of time on the towpath. Then there's a man on one of the computers and a woman reading the paper in an armchair, underneath the skylight. Nobody else, unless they're in the biographies section at the back.

I look at the big patch of sunlight, which falls right into the middle of the children's section. I can see the dust dancing in the air.

I wheel around, past Sam, and go outside and away from the door before I'm sick. I kneel on the pavement and press my face against the brick of a friendly house.

'You've built this up,' Sam says behind me. 'It's not that big a deal.'

'I know,' I snap into the bricks.

'If you're going to do this campaign or whatever ... I mean, it's absurd, but if you're going to waste your time you might as well use it to get over – this. Look, Dallas, you've just got to do it once, properly, and you'll be fine.'

I sit down. I'm tired of feeling so tired. Sam squats beside me. 'Where's Billy?' I ask.

'Ruby's got him. You know he hated going in there too – after. I had to drag him the first couple of times and he screamed his head off.'

'Yeah?'

'You have to reclaim it, that's all. It's basic. Like you.'

'What if I puke on the floor?'

'Then the ghost of your vomit will probably haunt the luxury-flat buyers for years to come. You're so emotional – you get that from her, but she never tried to hide it like you.'

We sit side by side on the pavement. Then he hauls me up.

'Ten minutes.'

'Two.'

'Ten.'

'Five?'

'Ten.' He puts his hand on my back and shoves me through the door.

'Dallas!' Gracie says, looking up from the floor. 'God but it's good to see you here again.' She starts getting up. It takes her a while and she has to lean on one knee. Gracie is pretty old. It probably is time she retired. Ruby is there in the kids' section too, reorganising the books Billy is throwing on the floor. She waves at me.

I sit down at the long table, where I never used to sit, and stare at the romance shelf. Romance writers have funny names. Then I turn my head and look at the door, and the steps.

'Come on,' I hear her saying. 'You and me. Changing the world. One leaflet at a time.'

'I don't want to change the world tonight.' That's what I said. 'I just want to read my book.'

'But Dall-as, it'll be you and me. Hanging out. Bonding.'

'Why would I want to hang out with you?' I was joking. But.

'I guess I'll go on my own then,' she said. 'Poor me.'

'Poor you,' I said, and I came in here. That was the last thing I said to her.

'Dallas,' Billy says at my knee, jolting me. 'Read me this.' It's *Mr Magnolia* in French. I stumble through it, while Gracie shows Ruby the comic books and Sam leans against the history shelf pretending not to watch me. It's nowhere near as bad as I thought, though I feel like a visitor. Trying to pronounce French words, while Billy tells me from memory what they mean, fills up my head and keeps the voices out. Sam's voice, telling me there's a taxi outside because we have to go to the hospital. Gracie, when she cried and said she'd be saying the rosary and that everything would be fine. And Billy screaming.

I look at the page and I read the book and I hold Billy's hand. And when we're done Sam says we can leave.

* * *

'Where have you been?' Violet squawks the second we step inside the door.

'The library,' I say. I feel proud of myself. I haven't felt proud of myself in ages.

'All of you?'

'Yeah.'

'What about me?'

I spend the evening looking up stuff about campaigning. Petitions, and leaflets, and letter-writing and stuff. There's no getting away from the fact that it's boring, but it's peaceful in our house for once. Gemma runs in and out with her arms full of washing. Violet is at the table too, wrestling with a fairy sticker book. Sam and Billy sit on the floor playing chess.

'You should probably start with a letter,' Gemma says, dropping a pair of pants on my head.

I groan. 'Who writes letters?'

'You know what I mean. An email, then, but formally expressed.'

'Who to?' Sam asks. 'Don't cheat, Billy. The prime minister? The Avengers? Ophelia Silk?'

Ophelia Silk is the enemy. Momma went out campaigning against her, but she was elected council leader in May of last year – just before they started talking about selling the library. When I think about it, if that hadn't happened Momma wouldn't have been out on her bike with a basket full of leaflets that evening. And I know that's unreasonable, but I also think that I'm not the only one thinking it right now. Sam checkmates Billy without realising what he's doing. Gemma clambers upstairs, dropping washing at every step.

'How y'all doing?' Jessi breezes in with a clanking carrier bag, lobbing a cigarette end over her shoulder into the darkness. 'Why so quiet? Who wants beer? How's my Billy? Jesus, Sam, you got the kid playing chess already?'

'He likes it,' Gemma says, coming back down.

'Sure he does. What's going on?'

I tell her. She listens with her head on one side while she wrenches the top off a beer bottle. 'So what's your first move?'

'Hand grenades at dawn,' Sam mutters.

'Gemma says we should write a letter to Ophelia Silk at the council,' I say.

'What the hell kind of a name is that? An open letter?'

'Not at first,' Gemma says, buttering bread for tomorrow's sandwiches. 'It's courteous to give her a chance to respond without forcing her. First.'

'Sounds like so much wasted time,' Jessi says, passing me a beer.

'Funny,' says Gemma, taking it off me.

Jessi passes me a Vimto instead. 'Of course, back in Texas, the protests and the campaigns tend to be a little crazier. More at stake. Real issues to fight about, like the death penalty – life and death . . .'

'So you're saying that here is infinitely better than there,' says Sam in a tight voice.

'Now, Sam,' says Gemma. 'I'm sure there are some good things about Texas.'

I say, 'I love Texas.' I do, too. I've been there three times in my life – that was always what we used to be saving for, flights to Texas – Austin with Jessi, and then the farm with Granma. I wonder if we'll ever go again. Jessi slings her arm over my shoulders.

'Tell the truth, Dallas, ain't you tempted to send it to the papers and make her squirm a little?'

'But the paper wouldn't publish it,' I say.

'They might,' Sam says from the floor. 'Not that it will make any difference. Sweet little schoolgirl bearding the council lion, you know the kind of crap they like to write about. It is kind of burning bridges though.'

'Burn 'em,' says Jessi, wiping her mouth.

'Give her a couple of days and then copy in the papers,' says Gemma, throwing the ham back in the fridge. 'I would suggest.'

'Time's a-wastin',' says Jessi.

'It doesn't matter, it's all pointless,' says Sam.

I'm glad we got that settled.

The library's not the only thing I've got to worry about either. I carry a stash of sanitary towels around in my school bag and wash my knickers in the sink – it's so hot they dry in twenty minutes on my windowsill. Nobody notices, and by Thursday morning it seems to have gone. Phew. I expect next month I'll be totally ready for it and it'll be fine.

But Friday's our transition day. When we all go to our new secondary school and get shown around and find out what forms we're in and have science lessons and stuff. Nobody at home seems bothered about it, which I suppose is understandable because everyone's thinking about Billy starting school in September. Billy and Violet's 'settle-in day' is in two weeks. Violet's in a state about it already.

'What shall I wear?' she asks, her blonde frizz appearing at the top of the ladder after she's supposed to be in bed, with this anxious expression on her face. 'No, in a minute, Mummy. Dallas, what shall I wear?'

'Kid, I feel you,' I could say, because I'm worried about the same thing. I hear Gemma soothing her, talking about her tutu skirt, and her head disappears again. I need to think on this because they don't have uniform at my new school. THEY DON'T HAVE UNIFORM AT MY NEW SCHOOL.

Friday's OK. I can muster something decent for Friday, if I plan my washing. Aiza will probably tell me what to wear anyway. But in September – what will I do? Will Gemma take me shopping? Momma would have taken me shopping. But I can't ask Gemma about it, she doesn't have time or money for stuff like this, and Jessi – I don't know if she even has a job to go back to, she keeps not talking about it.

I'd better get up in a minute and make sure I have something that's OK that isn't covered in grease. Things do end up tucked into my duvet or fallen down the side of my mattress instead of getting washed.

'Don't be stupid, Dallas,' says Aiza. 'As if they'd make you start school without buying you stuff. Ruby I'm worried about, but not you. Anyway, listen, it's no problem tomorrow, you can just wear your grey T-shirt that says "Summer Days" and those jeans shorts you've got with the stars on. Or if it's raining . . .'

I don't know why I ever worry. Everybody has everything covered.

'You're a very sarcastic person, Dallas,' Aiza says.

I write the letter. Gemma checks it for spelling, Jessi makes it more fiery, and Sam makes me rewrite it entirely with a different structure. I email it to Ophelia Silk. I also copy in our MP and the local paper, because like Jessi says, we don't have much time. Gemma doesn't make a fuss or anything. She's busy with work again, she's hardly said a word to me the last couple of days. Although she shouts at me when I don't bring Billy back from the meadow till past his bedtime. I don't cry this time. I'm tired of crying.

On Friday morning I'm actually nervous. And slow at everything, so that I end up joggling elbows with Violet at the sink, both of us brushing our teeth while Sam is trying to get Billy to pee. Our bathroom is tacked on to the side of the house so that you have to step outside the back door to go in and it's not very big – all blistered paint walls that shake if you sit down too hard. With four of us inside it's so steamed up I can't see my face in the mirror. 'Try being me,' says Violet, who can hardly see over the sink.

Today Billy's story is *The Giant Jam Sandwich*. 'Read it like Momma,' he says, and I blink at my blurry reflection. He doesn't mention Momma often. Sam starts reading in a daft German accent – Billy is thrilled, and Violet, who wasn't expecting it, nearly chokes herself on her toothbrush. By the end Billy is laughing so hard his laugh has gone completely silent, and Violet falls off her step. I can see Sam about to lose it too. Then we hear someone hammering on the door next to us.

'Oh Christ,' I say, after I've gagged on the toothpaste and wiped it off my T-shirt, 'that's Aiza.'

'Good luck,' Sam says, drying Billy's hands and Violet's face on the towel.

The boathouse isn't on Aiza's way but she said she didn't want to be hanging around waiting for me. We go together to Ruby's block of flats to pick her up, and then finally to the school, which is miles further than St John's, our primary. It feels like we've been walking for about fifty hours by the time we arrive.

'Right,' Aiza says, 'we've got to get you a bike, Rubes.'

'Mmm,' she says.

'And then you've got to learn to ride it.'

Ruby looks hurt. 'I only fall off when I go round corners.'

There are hordes of kids our age clustered outside Reception. A man comes out with a loudspeaker and starts telling us where to go. It's hard to listen because there's ten classes' worth of registers. Ruby gets called before me, trailing off behind Jake and Shanti who are in our year at primary. Finally he gets to me. I'm in 7SU. I haven't been listening so I jump, and also I miss the rest of the names. It doesn't include Aiza anyway. She's still sitting cross-legged on a patch of grass with her eyes shut, as if she's too cool to be interested in anything.

'Ah-izzer Hassan,' says the man with the loudspeaker, already well on to the next register before my new class has got itself inside – we're being held up by Gilbert Finch who's dribbling an invisible basketball. The loudspeaker man has already mutilated about fifty names.

'Aiza,' Aiza says sharply. As there's only twenty or so kids left sitting down, the man hears her.

'Sorry. Aiza.'

'Not a very good start, is it?' I can hear Aiza saying as I follow my class indoors.

'Are you in 7SU?' I ask Gilbert Finch.

'Yes, Dozy.'

Brilliant. Just me and Gilbert Finch.

A tall person – I can't decide whether he's a sixth-former or a teaching assistant or our teacher – leads us inside, and down a corridor that has a lot of paintings on the wall – again, can't decide if they're by actual artists or by people at the school. Through a courtyard, and up some steps, and then up a dark staircase, and suddenly we're in a long corridor with big white doors. 'This is the science block,' he says.

We all go through a door into an actual science lab, with a skeleton and everything. There is a smiley woman in there with a big chunky necklace. 'Hello!' she says. 'I'm Miss Upton. I'm going to be your form teacher in September. Everybody find a seat. Thank you, William,' she says to the tall person, who leaves.

I don't sit at the same table as Gilbert Finch but as he's at the next one and we're both sitting at corners, we're close. Which is both comforting and annoying.

Miss Upton takes the register. I look around the room but my eyes aren't quick enough to match up names with faces. The only one I manage is the weird one, a boy called Monty.

'Poor sucker,' says Gilbert Finch. 'Mind you, he looks like your type, Dallas.'

After that I talk to the people on my table, who are girls and are called Natalya, Grace and Keisha. They seem OK, especially Grace who has two thick plaits like Anne of Green Gables. We play some games till morning break, when William comes back and shows us the canteen. I am immediately grabbed and dragged into a corner by Aiza. 'How's it going and they all keep calling me Ah-izzer, it's making me doubt my authenticity,' she hisses. 'I'm in 7PW and I've got a bloke for a teacher again but he'll be easy, he's dead young. There's Ruby.'

Ruby looks pale. If we were at normal school today the teacher would definitely send her to the office.

'Are you all right?' I ask her.

'Yes,' she says. 'It's massive, isn't it. I'm not going to know where to go.'

'You will, in like a day. That's what everyone says,' says Aiza. 'My form room's a language room, it's got all this audio stuff and headphones everywhere.'

'I'm in a science lab,' I say.

Ruby cheers up fractionally. 'Me too.'

'We must be on the same corridor,' I say. 'Anyone in your form from St John's? I've got Gilbert Finch.'

We chat all breaktime. I don't know if it's what we're meant to do but I think everyone is sticking with their old friends as hard as they can – I can see little knots of people standing talking urgently to each other when they've probably sat on the same table for the last seven years. I'm even pleased to see Sophie when she wanders by, looking a bit lost without Libby. I wonder where Libby is today. I don't know if private schools do this whole settling-in thing on the same day as normal schools.

'Oh, Libby's back at St John's,' says Aiza. 'She's got to go in with the Year 5s for the day.'

'How do you know that?'

'Because I listen, Dallas,' she says. 'Why is everything such a mystery to you? "I'm Dallas, I never have a clue what's going on around me . . ."'

'What's wrong with you?' I ask.

She makes a face.

After break we go to the library. It's this huge round room with high ceilings, and tables and chairs, and books everywhere. It will take me a while to read my way through here – even if I start reading properly again. I stand at the first shelf – all children's fiction, authors beginning with A or B – and run my hands across the spines. I'd forgotten doing that. Some of the spines are soft as cotton, a few are bound in rough fabric and some are plasticky. My knuckles slide down the grooves on either side of a slim blue book that's a friendly size, and consider pulling it out to look at the back.

'Do you like reading?'

I jump and turn round. The librarian is right behind me. 'Sort of,' I say.

'Did you have a library at your primary school?'

'Sort of,' I say again, 'but it's in the corridor.'

'No librarian?'

'No. And they're shutting down our local library,' I say, without exactly meaning to.

She nods. 'I'm hoping somebody might stop it,' she says, 'or try to.'

And then of course I have to tell her about how my

stepmother and my aunt are trying to get me to be a library superhero.

'You should try and get your friends behind you,' she says, 'and people at your school.'

'Mmm,' I say, because how.

'Seriously. Young people are a huge resource in this kind of thing, you know, once you get them interested. Think about how hard it must be for a politician, or anyone, to say no to children who are asking not to have their books taken away.'

I say I'll think about it, and she seems pleased. I suppose she might be right, but how am I supposed to get them behind me? I'm not the Pied Piper of Hamelin.

Aiza is in a bad mood. At lunchtime she looks at the queue in the canteen and then marches us down to the school office, which is a lot bigger than the one at St John's. Ruby looks all around her, memorising where she should come when she cuts her finger on the first day.

'Excuse me,' says Aiza to the woman on the front desk.

'Yes?'

'My name is Aiza Hassan.'

'Yes?'

'I'm going to be in 7PW.'

'Mmm?'

'I'd like you to make a note on all the registers about how to pronounce my name correctly.'

'What?'

'It will spoil my start at school if I have to correct every single teacher on it,' she says. 'Not that it's that complicated. Surely you have some provision for this?'

Ruby and I back away a bit.

'What's wrong with Aiza?' I murmur.

Ruby frowns. 'I think it's her dad.'

In the afternoon we have a science lesson. We have to put on lab coats that smell of other people, but we do get to play with Bunsen burners and some stuff out of glass pots. I'm distracted when I look out of the window and see Ruby trailing across the football pitch with her new form. Gilbert Finch is working at the table behind me. 'What's up with Ruby?' he asks.

'I don't know,' I say.

I think about Ruby, and her mum, and her nan. Every once in a while her mum gets a bad boyfriend, or a bad break-up, and then she gets ill and Ruby always ends up living at her nan's house. But even when her mum's all right they argue, argue all the time. I've heard them. My mum and dad used to be a bit like that, but he wasn't there all that often. When she fought with Jessi it was worse. There was a nasty one a couple of years ago – Jessi said Momma wasn't really gay and Gemma was just a stopgap while Momma got over how rubbish my dad was – Momma kicked her out. But they were still talking on the phone two weeks later.

I hear a fizz and a startled yelp behind me, and Gilbert Finch says, 'Miss? Miss, I've set Dallas on fire.'

I must remember not to sit near Gilbert Finch in science lessons.

Miss gallops across the room and sprays me with a ton of foam out of a fire extinguisher. It's quite reassuring in a way, nothing got through the lab coat. All I lose is a few hairs and goodness knows I've got enough of them. She's still shouting when the bell goes for the end of the day. Keisha is picking burnt hair off my neck and Natalya is cleaning up for me.

'I was just testing it out,' Gilbert Finch says. 'That powder you gave us. And the Bunsen burner. And the lab coat.'

'You all right now?' Natalya asks me as we clatter down the stairs, leaving them to it. 'Not too singed? Fancy walking home together?' Natalya has long blonde hair and is wearing short pink dungarees. She goes to a primary school where they don't have uniform so maybe that's why she has an advanced style.

'Er, I said I'd meet a couple of my friends,' I say. We haven't talked – me and Aiza and Ruby – about how it's going to go with new people, even though realistically we knew we wouldn't be in the same class.

'Don't worry,' Natalya says. 'I've got my bike anyway. See you in September then.'

'Have a good summer,' we say at the same time, and laugh. It's weird. It suddenly feels real. In two and a half months we'll be here. And in five weeks we'll leave primary school for good.

'All right,' Aiza says. 'You two are the nosiest . . . All right. My dad sat me down last night and told me he wants me to meet his new *girlfriend*.'

Oh.

I don't remember how I felt when Momma told us she and Gemma were a couple. Mainly surprised; I don't think I minded.

'Is she moving in?' Ruby asks.

'*No*,' Aiza says, with pure disgust.

'What are you worried about?' I ask.

She looks at me like I'm thick. 'Hello. Gold diggers, anyone? Not to mention wicked stepmothers beating me up and making me scrub floors and stuff if she ever does move in.'

'I thought you had a cleaner,' says Ruby.

'It might not be serious,' I say.

'You think? But he's never told me about any of them before.' She sniffs. 'Let alone tried to get me to meet them.'

'Maybe only he likes her,' says Ruby hopefully. 'Maybe she's not serious about him.'

'Or,' I say, 'maybe it won't last. Look at Ruby's mum.'

'Yeah,' says Ruby. 'She's always got a bloke but it never lasts.'

'Ruby scares them off,' I say.

'I do,' nods Ruby.

'Great,' says Aiza. 'But doesn't your mum plummet into depression every time she breaks up with one of them?'

'Yeah,' says Ruby. 'But I think she would do that anyway. Actually it normally happens before they break up.'

'You're not making me feel better, guys,' says Aiza.

'How was it?' says Gemma. 'Did you behave yourself? Can you make a quick salad while you're in here? I've just got to peg the washing out.'

'How was it?' asks Sam. 'Who's your form teacher – oh, Miss Upton – well at least she's not a PE teacher. Can you give Billy's hands a wash while you're up?'

'How was it?' asks Jessi. 'Any sexy boys there?'

'How was it?' asks Violet. 'Did you get a best friend?'

Wish I'd stayed at yrs I text.

Me 2 adds Ruby a moment later.

No reply from Aiza.

6

'You've had an email, Dallas,' Gemma says when I get in from school.

'What? Who from?'

'A certain Ophelia Silk.'

'What?' says Sam.

'Who?' says Jessi.

'Oh God,' I say.

It turns out she wants to meet me, and my 'team', at four o'clock on Friday. Sam scoffs at this and asks if she knows it's me and only me and I haven't read a book in eight months. Gemma says it's fine, she'll move her meetings around and come with me, and we can ask Gracie, and maybe Jessi . . . Jessi instantly says of course she'll be there.

I ask if I have to go, if they can't just do it without me. Gemma says no, they can't.

Jessi slings an arm across my shoulder. 'As if you aren't ready. Hell, this is all your idea.'

'It's all on you, Dallas,' says Sam. 'How's it feel?'

'I can't believe it,' I'm telling Aiza and Ruby as we drop our phones off in the office the next morning. 'Me at a council meeting. I can't decide if it sounds more boring or terrifying.'

'Terrifying,' says Ruby.

'Boring,' says Aiza.

'Oh God,' I say.

'Why are you going to a council meeting?' Ms Wilson asks, picking up her mug of tea before Aiza's bag knocks it off the desk.

'About the library,' I say. 'To try and stop them shutting it down.'

'That's great,' Ms Wilson says. 'Put Libby's phone back, Aiza. When are you going, Dallas?'

'Friday,' I say gloomily. 'Straight from school.'

'Friday?' Aiza slams the drawer shut.

'Good luck with it,' Ms Wilson says. 'Let us know how it goes. Maybe you could do an assembly about it.'

'Friday?' Aiza says again, marching us out. 'What about the sleepover?' Aiza's dad's away so she's asked me and Ruby round to save her from having to talk to the babysitter.

'I'll still come,' I say. 'Straight after.'

'You better.'

'Having a sleepover, kids?' Libby says, behind us as usual. 'How cute.'

'I suppose you're going nightclubbing,' I say. I'm not in the best of tempers, but I've got nothing on Aiza today.

* * *

'Have you told your dad how you feel about his girlfriend?' Ruby asks Aiza at break.

'Yeah.'

'Well? What did he say?'

'OK, I haven't.'

'Aiza!'

'Don't pick on me, Rubes. I'm not in the mood.'

Ruby scrapes her hand on the wall again, and gets sent to the office for an ice pack. I'm not feeling chatty, and neither is Aiza, so we just sit against the tree. Then the football comes skittering over towards us, with Gilbert Finch following it.

'Hey, Aiza,' he says, hooking it in with his left foot and stopping for a second. 'I saw your dad in town the other night with some seriously fit bird.'

'What?' I say.

'Di-vine. Your dad's the man.'

Aiza waves a wasp away wearily.

'She might be nice,' I say when he's gone.

'I don't care if she's nice, Dallas,' Aiza says without opening her eyes. 'I don't want her around.'

'Why not?' I say, a bit more crossly than I mean it to come out, but *honestly*.

'She just doesn't,' Ruby says, cradling her ice pack. I wonder if they've been talking about this without me.

'I know what you mean and everything, but you're being stupid.'

'Oh shut up, Dallas,' says Aiza.

'You can't care that much, you're just looking for something to have a tantrum about,' I say. I know families are hard but you have to try to fix things, not just sulk. Families are worth fixing. If I could do anything at all, or say anything, or put up with anyone anywhere and have my mother back too, I'd do it in a second. In a heartbeat. Naked, if I had to.

'You don't know what you're on about.'

'It isn't real. You're just *acting*,' I say, before I know I'm going to say it.

'I know nobody is allowed to feel sad except you,' Aiza says, and she gets up and walks off.

The whistle goes then which is great because it means I don't have to decide what to do. We sit on the same table, by ourselves, and it's embarrassing, but we're only watching a DVD, so I shove my chair back against the cold radiator and don't look at anybody. Of course Aiza has the right to feel sad, but it's not as if her mum hasn't always been missing, and she's had years and years of her dad to herself, and she hasn't even met this woman. Who might be lovely, or at least normal.

After Momma died, I went to see this therapist a few times. We all did, they said we had to, well Billy had a different one but we all had to talk to somebody. She said that some people eat grief whole. That's really what she said. She said it was something you had to make part of you, in the end, if you were ever going to get over it, and that some people were able to eat some griefs whole, and it was probably more painful that way but maybe they could digest it quicker in the end. But she said I might not be able to, sometimes people couldn't. 'You might be too young,' she said, 'or you might not be built that way, or it might not be the right kind of grief.'

I don't think it was the right kind of grief. But I ate some big bits of it all the same. And I knew what she meant, sometimes it was like that pain where you eat a sandwich too fast – or you eat a sandwich made by Sam, who basically likes to cut a loaf of bread into about three slices – and it gets stuck in your chest and you think you'll be sick or it will cut your insides before you can swallow it.

I still get lumps of it. I didn't much like the day our SATs finished, and everybody but me was really happy . . .

Some parts come back, which seems unfair; I shouldn't have to keep trying to swallow the same bits. There's an irritating crumb of grief that I cough on practically every time I come home to the boathouse and my mother isn't there.

Ruby reaches over and hands me her ice pack. It's barely cold any more but I lean my cheek on it anyway. Aiza passes me a green Nerd from her pencil case without looking. Those Nerds have been in there for weeks, possibly months, and it tastes of pencil shavings. Ruby gets an orange one.

'What's up with you anyway, Dallas?' Aiza asks later.

'Nothing. All right, stop that.' I push her away. 'I'm just worried about the library.'

'Ruby,' says Aiza, 'we have to fix Dallas.'

Ruby sucks her finger. 'Why don't you get a petition?'

'That's a brilliant idea,' said Aiza. 'Rubes, you're a constant surprise to me. Dallas, you need to get a petition. Then you take it into your meeting on Friday and say . . .'

'But how would I get it?' I ask. 'Especially by Friday? I mean, I don't think Gemma would let me go round knocking on doors, so how am I going to get anyone to sign?'

'That is hard,' says Aiza. 'Let me think. Where could we possibly hope to find a bunch of people who use Queen Street library?'

'Oh yeah,' I say.

Ms Wilson lends us some paper, and then when I look sad she types it up for us, and lets me text Gemma and Sam to tell them we're going to the library after school.

It's not, like, madly successful, but it's a lot more successful than it would have been if I'd gone on my own and spent hours standing on one leg waiting for a good moment to approach people. Aiza just marches up to them. She makes them fill out the section for 'why this library is important to me' too, which is technically optional.

'Stop reading, Dallas,' she says, marching back after forcing an old lady wearing earmuffs to sign. 'This is meant to be your petition.'

'No it's not,' I say, hastily sliding the book back on to the shelf. 'The library's everyone's, that's the point.'

'So go and make your point.' She shoves me towards a man in a suit who's hiding behind the self-help shelf. He says he's just come in out of the rain, which is a light sprinkle at most, and he doesn't think libraries have much place in the modern world. 'I mean, this one isn't even open on Wednesday afternoons.'

I stare at him, trying to understand his point. 'But if it shuts,' I say, 'it won't be open any afternoons.'

I hear Gracie laughing behind me.

He signs in the end. I think we get everybody who comes in between three thirty and five forty-five to sign. The trouble is that's only seventeen people, even counting toddlers.

'Leave it with me, girls,' says Gracie. 'Now, Ruby, let's have a look at that book I was telling you about.'

'Ruby doesn't like books,' Aiza tells her.

'All that means is she hasn't found the right ones yet,' says Gracie. 'Be a couple of dotes, would you, girls, and put those returned books back on the shelf, while I show Ruby the graphic novels? I got a great one in the other day about a wee girl called Hilda . . .'

Gemma does a clear-out of the big wardrobe, and the dark place under the boathouse where we shove things we're bored of, and she finds the big parasol and the cushions and sets up our little piece of garden. I forgot how nice it was to have the extra space. She even finds a string of solar-powered coloured lights that someone gave Momma which she never got round to putting up – Momma said she thought it might be light pollution and harmful to owls and stuff, but I think she just couldn't be bothered. It's nice.

'Do you think Billy would miss me if I died?' I ask Sam. We're outside. It's late but still light enough to paint our nails. Billy picks out a colour and I do one of his toes. That way I also get to do my own.

I look over at Sam and he's looking at me strangely. Guy Clark is playing on his phone – 'She Ain't Going Nowhere, She's Just Leaving'. 'What kind of question is that?'

'Well –' I do Billy's last nail green, trying not to get any on the rest of his toe – 'I mean, obviously he'd miss *you*. But . . . if I was gone, if I died now or I was already dead, do you think he'd mind when he was older. Like say eleven. If he couldn't remember me.'

'He'd remember you,' Sam says. He flips over a page of his book. Billy gravely rests his head on top of mine for a couple of seconds. He has a very heavy head.

'Are you looking forward to university?' I ask. Every now and again I remember that Sam is going to be gone soon. But I don't think about it much because I can't possibly imagine what it'll be like.

'Not really,' he says. 'Anyway, you know I'm probably not going.'

'Gemma says you are.'

'I know she does.'

'What does Prue say?' I bet she agrees with Gemma. That's probably why she hasn't been around lately, because he knows they'd gang up on him.

'Aren't you full of questions?' He puts his book down. 'Pass us the purple.'

It's nice, just the three of us outside, listening to music and everything, with Lonesome coming over and rolling around between us. It's almost a shame when Gemma comes out. She doesn't order us in or anything, even though I heard Violet having a tantrum twenty minutes ago over how come she had to go to bed when Billy got to sit outside having his nails done.

'Say what you will about the house,' Gemma says, looking up at the sky and breathing in, 'it's not a bad place to live, this little patch of land. I mean, who could ask for more, right?'

'Maybe,' I say.

'It wouldn't kill me to have a couple of extra bedrooms,' Sam says.

'Oh come on, you two! How can you criticise on a night like this?'

'If Jessi was here,' Sam says, 'she'd say only Texas nights are even tolerable.'

I laugh too, even though when I think of a Texas night on Granma's farm, with the moon like a great big wheel in the sky instead of the lemon slice you get here, and bright stars, and campfire sparks, and space – it gives my heart a knock.

'We should be kinder to Jessi,' says Gemma. 'She's picking the kids up from nursery for me on Friday.'

Sam sits upright. 'She's what?'

'Well, you're going to that exhibition with Prue, and it turns out I couldn't get out of my meeting, so Jessi said she'd get them.'

'But she'll lose them,' said Sam. 'Or sell them.'

'Don't be silly. Anyway it's only for an hour.'

'I'm amazed she offered,' he mutters.

'I think she was pleased to,' Gemma says. 'I can't imagine what she's doing with herself all day, with only that tent to come back to and nobody to look after.' She gazes up at the stars. 'Bless her.'

Libby's doughnut this week is blueberry cheesecake.

'I mean, that is absolutely ridiculous,' says Aiza, sitting back down in her seat after craning to look at it. 'I've never even had blueberry cheesecake, let alone a blueberry cheesecake doughnut.'

'I've had blueberry cheesecake,' Ruby says, with a sigh.

'No you haven't.'

'I have! My mum brought it home from the pub last Friday. She said it was leftovers.'

We all stare for a few seconds at Libby's back, as she delicately licks the purple off her fingers. Which is a mistake, because Jada, across the table from her, notices and nods towards us. Libby turns round and her hair goes *swish*.

'Eyeing up my lunch *again*, girls? Do your yoghurts not match up?'

'Actually,' Aiza says as we start to leave, 'we were wondering if your mother was going to carry on this cute tradition when you're at big school. Buying special treats in stripy bags for her precious baby girl?'

Libby flushes. 'At least I've got a mother.'

I get in Ruby's way, mostly on purpose. Unexpectedly though Aiza throws her lunchbox straight into Libby's face and then jumps on top of her.

It's been a while since any of us was in headteacher trouble. Ruby and I spend most of the afternoon sitting in the office, missing PE, which I can't say I mind. Aiza comes out of the headteacher's room. She looks at us and shrugs. 'They just told me to come and sit down. I think they're talking about me.' She looks sideways at Ruby, who's sitting with her elbows on her knees, looking at her feet, and hasn't glanced up. Aiza looks at me, and this time I shrug. 'What's up, Rubes?'

Now Ruby shrugs.

'Are you all right?' I ask. I'm asking them both.

Aiza laughs. 'Course I am. What can they do to me? We're Year 6, aren't we, it's not like we're even really here any more. Are we, Ruby? Ruby.' She nudges her knee. 'Ruby.'

'Sorry about Libby,' Ruby says.

'What are you sorry for?'

'Her. What she said.'

'You're weird,' Aiza tells her.

'It's not your fault, Ruby,' I add.

'Yeah. But.'

Aiza puts her arm round Ruby's shoulder, just briefly. 'It doesn't even matter,' she says. 'We're all managing fine, aren't we?'

We sit in a row, thinking about that.

Aiza's dad arrives in the office, with Miss Whittle, the SENCO, next to him. They stand looking down at us; they look like giants from down here. 'Aiza,' he sighs.

Aiza bursts – like a dam, like pictures you see on the news of huge tidal surges – into tears. She says something that her dad and Miss Whittle don't understand, not at first, because it's under a tidal surge of water, but Ruby and I know she's saying: 'I don't want a new mother'.

I meet Jessi outside Boots. She gives me two bottles of nail varnish. The kids look all smeared, and I try to wipe Billy's face. 'What's this round your mouth, Billy?'

'Toffee,' he says happily.

'Toffee?'

'Coffee,' Jessi says off-handedly. 'I took them to the Grand Café.'

'You gave them coffee?' I ask.

'Not me,' Violet says scornfully. 'I had Coke.'

I 'hmm'. 'I don't know if Gemma's going to like Billy having coffee,' I say.

'But I liked it,' Billy tells me. 'Toffee is great.'

Jessi tousles my hair. 'I ain't afraid of Gemma, Dallas.'

When we get to the council buildings, Gemma's pacing up and down outside and Gracie is talking to the trombone player from the brass band, which always seems to be playing outside Marks and Spencer.

'You're almost late,' Gemma says, literally spitting on a tissue and wiping my face with it. 'Come on, we've got to get to the third floor.' She looks at me and straightens my bunches. Then she sweeps us into the town hall, which is all black and mirrored on the outside.

Jessi pulls my left bunch crooked again while we're waiting for the lift.

The meeting doesn't go well. To begin with it's just the five of us and Gracie and a woman called Daisy who's the councillor who normally looks after libraries. And she seems quite nice. I mean, it's like a chat, she knows Gracie already and they talk about some new librarian over at Wheatley who's doing something new and disgraceful like having an erotica shelf or something – that's when I start listening but I've missed the beginning.

'You wouldn't see it in an X-rated film,' says Gracie, 'and didn't she seem like such a lovely girl when she first got the job . . .'

'Lovely,' agrees Daisy, 'you really wouldn't have foreseen any interest in unnatural things like that.'

'Ladies,' says Gemma, and then the door bangs open and Ophelia Silk is standing there in a bright blue suit and a bright pink face with another woman behind her carrying her cup of coffee and we have to start all over again.

The worst part of it is she actually asks me what I'm doing there and what I want to say. Jessi says after that this is what fascists and dictators do – they pretend to give a voice to the voiceless in a situation where they hold all the power, and then they can say the opposition have had every chance, and Gemma says that there's an easy remedy and that's to be prepared and we should try it next time.

Because I'm not very good at it.

'Er,' I say. 'I don't want the library to shut down.'

'This library in particular?'

'Well . . .'

'Or libraries in general?'

'Well. Libraries in general I suppose.'

'Because you know libraries are closing down all over the country.'

I watch Gemma wrestling with Billy, who wants the sound up on his DS. 'I think . . . I sort of think that's a shame.'

She nods her head fast. 'I so agree, it is a shame. It is a shame. They're a lovely idea. And can you tell me – just, in whatever words come to you – exactly why libraries, or this library, why you think it matters?'

'Er . . .'

I mean, who doesn't understand why libraries are good and why we should keep them open?

'Because there are so so many worthy and wonderful causes out there, and very sadly there just isn't very much money at the moment, is there? I mean, what would you say, yourself, Dallas – can I call you Dallas, is that OK? – if I were to say, let's see, if I were to say that here's the money, here's the amount of money we have, and we have this and this and this we have to spend it on, like schools, and then this last little bit we have left, we could spend it either on another library, or we could use it for helping young people who have poor mental health, for instance, or disabilities?'

Gemma coughs.

The worst of it is that she sits there, Ophelia Silk, with her coffee in front of her and her weird static Lego hair, looking at me and nodding understandingly even though I'm not saying anything, and then she takes notes, and all in all treats me like I'm brilliant. It's Gemma and Jessi who are shuffling their feet and fidgeting. And I know I'm messing it all up and that every time she smiles and 'mmm's she's doing up another screw on the lid of the coffin she's put our library in.

'I do understand it's terribly sad for the few people, I'm sure including yourselves –' she moves her hand around in the air – 'who do use the library often. And goodness knows we want to do what we can to serve our residents, and to serve minorities, including small-library users, but sometimes, sadly, the bottom line is . . .'

'But,' I manage at last, and she immediately stops talking and angles her head at me as if she doesn't want to risk missing what I say, 'what about the flats? The luxury flats?'

She sits back in her chair and sips her coffee. 'What about them?'

'You're making money out of closing down the library,' I say. Jessi clears her throat and gives me a thumbs up.

'*I'm* not making money, Dallas, goodness.' She laughs and puts down her coffee cup. 'The council is using its assets, it's true, and I think we can all agree that since we can't afford to keep the library open, it would be silly to leave it there closed when there are so many people needing housing in our city, no, let me finish, and when the council is, unfortunately, so short of money and with so many calls on our very limited budget.'

'I think Dallas feels,' says Gemma, looking at me to check I don't mind her speaking, and I don't mind so much I almost faint with relief, 'as we all do, that it would be an enormous shame to lose our well used library just to facilitate more expensive flats being built.'

'For rich people,' I add.

''Cause the rich bastards have taken enough, wouldn't you say?' Jessi says, looking at her threateningly. 'They've already taken the past and the present, are we going to let them have the future too?'

'Jessi!' hisses Gemma.

'Mmmm,' says Ophelia Silk.

'Did she say a rude word?' Violet asks.

'I guess you're one of them yourself, ain't you, lady,' says Jessi. 'Invested as hell in keeping the poor in their place. Ears closed to the cry of the poor as you stomp on their faces . . .'

Billy hits Violet on the head with his Nintendo DS. The meeting draws to a close after that.

'Thank you so much for coming in,' Ophelia Silk says, shaking my hand first. 'It's been so interesting, I've listened with such interest to your point of view. It's absolutely great to know there are children your age out there who feel so passionately about things. Of course as you know we have many many priorities on the council, and every one of them has people who feel strongly about them, but I will be certain to pass on your thoughts to my colleagues, and rest assured we'll be bearing them in mind when we make our final decision.'

'It hasn't been made yet then?' Gemma says.

She just smiles.

'Ow!' Gemma yells, because Billy has bitten her on the leg. She grabs him with one hand while she rubs the place with the other. Ophelia Silk has swept out. 'Billy, that was naughty. That hurt Gemma, do you understand?'

'Don't yell at him,' I tell her. 'He's just bored.'

'And full of coffee,' Violet adds.

'Full of *what*?'

7

Aiza's dad is just coming downstairs doing up his cufflinks as I arrive. He's wearing a shirt so sharp you could cut gingerbread with it. 'You're a pair of lifesavers, girls,' he says. 'Are you sure you're not afraid of all the ghosts?'

'What ghosts? No,' says Ruby. She coughs. I think she's having a reaction to his aftershave.

'Heroes. I'll be back later but I'm sure you'll be tucked up and fast asleep by then.'

'Go away, Dad,' says Aiza.

We leave the babysitter in the living room and go to Aiza's bedroom.

'What episode are we on?' Ruby asks, struggling with the box set.

'Did you see him?' Aiza says, in a voice that makes me stop halfway through opening a can of Coke (which naturally means that the ring pull comes off in my hand).

'Your dad?'

'I don't know who this woman is but she's turned him into a babbling, pink-shirted fool.'

'Your dad always looks like that,' I say, looking down at my unopenable can.

'What kind of woman likes a man who wears a pink shirt?'

Ruby considers this. 'I would have said more purple.'

'Puce,' I suggest.

'Focus, girls,' says Aiza. 'I need to find out what kind of woman this is.'

So Aiza has decided to do some online stalking, and because she's a weird computer-phobe I have to do it for her. 'I don't know how,' I protest.

'Oh come on, Dallas, use your imagination.'

'I mean, I could google her or whatever, but what do you think is going to come up?'

'It could be anything,' she says darkly. 'We'll start with Facebook.'

'None of us are on Facebook, we're only eleven.'

'Don't be so defeatist,' says Aiza. 'Oh, Dallas, just have a different can.' She chucks one at me. I don't catch it and it clonks me on the shin. 'You must know Sam's login.'

'Oh God,' I say. 'He'll kill me.'

'How will he know?' asks Ruby, stabbing the top of my first can of Coke with Aiza's nail scissors.

'Are you girls all right in there?' the babysitter calls ten minutes later.

'Yes,' Aiza calls back, rolling her eyes. 'Can you imagine,' she mutters, 'she's getting paid minimum wage, she should at least open the door and check we're not taking drugs or something. Now, look at this.'

We've found the right Sofia Rahman, at least we think it's the right one. 'Who has this many friends?' Aiza mutters. 'At her age?' She lives in Oxford. There are a lot of photos.

'I feel weird about this,' I say, draining my Coke. 'You've never even met her, shouldn't you meet her before you start stalking her?'

'Shut up, Dallas,' Aiza says, leaning over my shoulder. 'Besides, if she doesn't have the sense to keep her page private she deserves to be stalked. How old would you say she is?' Her forehead is furrowed. She leans into the screen and then away, squinting.

'I don't know,' Ruby says. 'She looks quite young in that one, but she could almost be thirty in that one.'

'Thirty?' Aiza says grimly. 'She's not thirty. Possibly twenty-five.'

'Well, how old's your dad?' I ask, reaching for the chocolate. 'He's not that old.'

'Thirty-four. He's thirty-four. He should not be dating . . .'

'Dollybirds?' Ruby suggests.

'Dollybirds. Thank you, Rubes. It's pathetic.'

'You don't know she's a dollybird,' I object, 'whatever that is. She might be really high-powered.'

'It doesn't even say if she works.'

Aiza throws herself in a scowling heap on her bed. Ruby trots next door to Aiza's own sugar-pink bathroom to run herself a bubble bath, which is something we both like to do when we stay over at Aiza's house. Neither of us has a bath at home.

I'm left sitting at the desk, and since Aiza clearly needs to sulk, I leave Sofia Rahman to herself and go back to Sam's profile page.

There's not that much to learn about my brother here, or not without hours to search. He doesn't seem to post often. There's the odd photo – one of the day they finished their A levels, and Sam has his head on the table in a pool of beer. He's wearing his Lone Star T-shirt. I remember thinking it was weird that he put that on to go out and celebrate – he's had it about a million years and it's dead scruffy, he used to wear it when we watched movies at home. Momma used to call it his loungewear. He doesn't look very happy considering it's a celebration.

Some of Prue's posts are dotted about. I like Prue. I like the way she looks, with orange hair about an inch long all over her head and millions of freckles. Her most recent post says she's just booked a ticket – Yay!!! – for Thailand and Vietnam and Cambodia. In October. I didn't know about that.

Is Sam going with you? one of her friends asks below the post. 'Dallas.'

Aiza's voice, sharp as usual, wakes me from the trance.

'What are you doing?'

'Nothing,' I say, shutting down the screen. 'Just pointless stalking.'

* * *

We watch a film, which Aiza keeps interrupting, and then eventually they fall asleep. I go into the bathroom for a while.

Last autumn when Momma had just died, my friends were really good to me. It wasn't like we talked about it or anything, I didn't want to, but they would let me just sit. But after a while I knew that couldn't go on forever, so I started trying to be funny again, so that they could be. Momma used to say, if you have to do something hard or yucky, pretend to be someone else while it's happening – most of the time I couldn't do that, but I could with them. Fake it through until you make it true. And I did, and it helped. I can be OK with them like I can't at home. But if I stay too long it gets too much.

At home on Saturday, things are uncomfortable. Gemma is cross that Jessi misbehaved in the council meeting, and also that she fed Billy coffee, and Jessi is cross back.

'I'm not a child,' Jessi mutters, 'and she's not the school principal, or the queen.'

'You totally sabotaged that meeting,' Gemma says. 'Now we'll never know what we could have achieved.'

'We do know. Nothing,' says Sam, trying to get Billy to hold a pen.

'We'll just have to move ahead with plans for a protest,' Gemma says.

'About time,' says Jessi.

'Completely and utterly pointless,' Sam says.

I wish up and down that they'd all shut up, or maybe ask me what I think since they all keep going on about this being my campaign. So I go upstairs. When I come down at least they've moved on to talking about Sam's prom, which is tonight. It's like it's a safe subject, for everyone but Sam who growls when anyone brings it up. He didn't enjoy the Year 11 one much. Then he brightens up a bit and says at least there's a bar this time round.

Jessi takes us shopping and tries to make Sam buy a fancy shirt, and then a silk tie. In the second-hand shop she wraps him in this weird black dinner jacket with shiny lapels, so that she can take pictures to send Granma. Sam says he only came out to get a proper coffee, but he ends up with a yellow tie – I made Prue tell me what colour her dress was. What I really wanted to ask her was how come she's going to Asia without Sam and Sam didn't tell us – unless he might be going with her, but he'd have said. And Jessi takes us to the florist to get a corsage, but the florist says we should have ordered a week ago. Sam says Prue won't care, so Jessi buys me a pair of grey and gold shorts and a baseball cap, and we get strawberry milkshakes in McDonald's because really even Sam prefers that to coffee.

Then we go home and Gemma produces a corsage in a box that she picked up for Prue.

'This is tragic,' Sam says, holding it between finger and thumb. 'She'll hate it.'

'If she hates it, she doesn't have to wear it,' Gemma says. 'But I bet she'll think it's nice you got it for her.'

He grunts, and sits down to play snakes and ladders with Billy.

I think the grown-ups are longing for this to be more of a big deal than it is. Jessi asks if Sam is having a fancy car, which is ridiculous. They both sit and twitch while he's getting showered and then upstairs getting ready. After a while he yells down to me to come up and trim his right sideburn.

I concentrate. I don't want to slice off part of his ear or trim him bald, not on prom night. His hair is still wet but the curl is kicking in. 'Want me to straighten it?' I ask, checking the other side to make sure I'm matching.

'As if,' he says. 'You'd burn it off. Like in *Little Women*.'

I giggle. 'I always knew you identified with Meg.'

'Shut up, Dallas.'

'You're Meg, you just admitted it.'

'You shouldn't be reading that stuff any more. You want classics, I'll line them up for you.'

'Leave me alone. I haven't even read it in months anyway.' I wipe the scissor blades off on his T-shirt. 'There, you're done.'

When he comes downstairs, ready to go, he almost looks handsome. Jessi's picking at her eyelashes and even Gemma looks as if she might like to cry, so naturally Sam gets cross and won't pose for any pictures, so it all gets a bit tetchy as usual. I'm the only one not wittering about photographs and I'm the only one who gets any – one of him and Billy, and one of him getting on his bike. Billy got a bit speechless when he saw Sam all dressed up. Even Violet is quiet, and I see her gawking out of the window as he's leaving.

After he's gone I send both the pictures to Granma, so that she'll have them. Somebody ought to be keeping this stuff for when we're old and we want to remember.

Jessi drinks white wine and puts on *The Last Picture Show*, then Gemma gets back in from washing Violet and says it's totally unsuitable for anyone under the age of thirty, which I have to say seems true, so to save a scrap I say I'll read to Billy.

'What story do you want?' I ask him.

He hands me *Where the Wild Things Are*, and I roll him over so I can lie down beside him and hold the book up for both of us to see – not that I don't know it off by heart.

'The night Billy wore his wolf suit,' I start, 'and made mischief of one kind and another . . .'

I don't go back down after. It's probably mean – Gemma and Jessi don't like each other – but I don't care tonight. I just want to go to bed.

I read for a while. Past when I'm meant to, even on a Saturday. When I come to the end of the book (*Claudine at St Clare's*, Sam would have a fit, but at least I know no tragedy is going to jump out at me) I turn over and look through the window for a while. The moon is shining right in. Momma used to bring Billy in here on nights like this, back when he was a little baby, and we'd read him *Goodnight Moon* together. And then we'd lie here, all three of us, till Billy fell asleep and sometimes I did too, and always when I'd wake up after, Momma would have left something here for me – her hairclip or something like that.

I don't seem to want to sleep. Long after Gemma checks on Billy and me I'm still awake, and somehow not surprised when Jessi comes tiptoeing into my room. 'Dallas?' she whispers.

'What?'

She scoots into bed with me. 'Move over, I'm cold.'

'How can you be cold?' I ask, moving over.

'I'm used to a hundred degrees at this time of year,' she says, huddling. 'How are you doing, Dallas?'

I sigh.

'Sam looked handsome.'

I agree that he did, relatively.

'Soon going to be your prom. We'll have to get you the dress of your dreams.'

'It's not for seven years,' I point out. 'We've got time.'

'Yeah.' She lies flat on her back. 'It's stuff like tonight – when I think about how jumpy your momma'd be – so proud – I remember her prom, you know that? Don't recall a thing about mine. But for hers, I went with her to buy the dress and all, and I put her hair up . . . she looked like a rose. It's nights like this when I know I'm still going to be missing her in ten years. And probably when I die.'

98

I stare up at the ceiling over my face.

'Gemma's wrong, you know,' she says. 'Saying how Rosie hated Texas.'

'It was Sam who said that,' I point out.

'Or maybe – but she loved it too. I couldn't believe it when she took off for *Oxford*. I guess I never knew before that how much it meant to her, being smart – more than I did. Oh, it took a long time to forgive her, Dallas. Maybe I haven't yet. It was even worse when she called and said she was pregnant and she was sticking around in England, then she was getting married.

'I'll never understand why she stayed here. Even when she finally left your daddy. And then I thought – maybe once you all were grown ... I never thought she'd fall for somebody else.'

I stare at her profile. I know what it's like to be disappointed with your family, even when it's not fair to be.

'And then she went and died.'

I wait. For morning, possibly.

'None of it matters any more, whether I can be grown up enough to forgive her for any of it, or to realise she didn't do nothing to me at all – because I can feel what you're thinking. She went and died on me.'

My bed used to be a safe place. I suddenly hear Lonesome purring somewhere; he must have sneaked in. I consider getting down to the bottom of the bed, where he is, where nobody can get at him.

She turns suddenly towards me. 'You're all I got left of her now, Dallas. Your momma was the most vivid thing I had in my life, you know?'

I know. 'But I'm not like that,' I say.

'You listen: sometimes I think you're not, you're so much quieter than her, and then I'll turn around and you'll be looking so like her I jump. And those texts you used to send me, all spring, it was like she was still here. That's why I came. I knew how like her you were getting. You and I got to hang on to each other, you hear me?'

I lie awake after Jessi weaves out again, stubbing her toe on my bag of nail varnishes which I left out because I didn't expect people to be wandering in and out of my room in the dark. I think about how funny it is that Momma and Jessi should look alike and sound alike but be so different, and how Momma used to cry after she spoke to Jessi on the phone because she missed her so much . . .

I think I must have fallen asleep because when my phone bleeps I nearly swallow my tongue. It's a WhatsApp message from Aiza, who is staying with her cousins in London tonight.

Guys it says. *Im locked in bathroom which is weirdly freezing cold with my dads phone*

Why Ruby says before I've finished reading Aiza's message. Does nobody sleep at night except me?

So I can have a look yeah. He thinks if its password protected he can keep me out?

What u looking 4 asks Ruby. It's a reasonable question. I look at my alarm clock. It's 1.45.

Look at this

Then there's a blurry picture of Aiza's dad, with a woman. A girl I suppose you might say, though she looks more grown-uppy than she did in most of her Facebook shots. They're grinning in a 'heyyy' kind of a way at the camera. She is pretty. As I'm wondering what to say Ruby flashes back a *Pretty so what*

A few seconds' silence and then *Just doing my due diligence Rubes*

I was asleep I complain.

Dont be such a square Dallas

I lie back on my pillow, picturing a square Dallas. I am quite square, but at least I don't have corners – I imagine myself with them, like a Lego person . . .

Girls

Another picture. Of a text message saying *See you later babe. I love you.* And a heart.

What am I going to do

I try to call, hoping that my face won't melt into my pillow. Hoping that Ruby will have got to her first. Whether or not she has, it's going straight to answerphone, and while I'm thinking about what a good friend would do, I fall asleep.

'Dallas. Dallas.'

I don't open my eyes. It can't possibly be morning, and it's even less possible that somebody else is trying to stop me sleeping.

'Dallas.'

If it's really Sam, he's being unusually patient. I open my eyes and recoil so fast I thump my head on the wall – his face is only about two centimetres away from where mine was.

'Sorry,' he says, sitting down suddenly. The mattress flumps.

'What is it?' I ask, rubbing my head.

'You have to get up and help me.'

'Help you what?'

'Dallas,' he says, slurring. 'Do you remember when Billy was a baby and never ever slept and Momma was tuckered out all the time and then she got flu? She couldn't get out of bed for two weeks? We did OK, didn't we?'

I do remember. There was a lot of watching films and eating pizza and sandwiches all day, the three of us tucked up on the sofa while Momma slept upstairs. We even went to the shops, when we ran out of food.

'We were fine, weren't we?' he says. 'We could manage, couldn't we?'

'Yes,' I say. 'But Momma was just upstairs.'

His face catches the moonlight from the window. It's wet.

'Are you OK? Was the prom good?'

'Not really. Will you come and see Billy?'

'Why?'

'He's awake and I'm too drunk,' he says. He tries to get up and then sits back down. 'I don't want to wake Gemma.'

I clamber out of bed. My legs are heavy. I can hear Billy now – cheeping. 'Come on then.'

'All right, coming,' he says, climbing into my bed as I reach the door.

Billy seems happy enough to see me, in the green light from his dinosaur night light. 'Want some water,' he says, bouncing on his pillow. 'Want some water, want some water.'

I get some. It means creeping downstairs and right through the sitting room past Violet's corner and Gemma's curtains. I bring up two glasses, and before I go back to Billy I take one in and leave it beside my bed for Sam.

I tuck Billy back into bed, and scramble into Sam's. Billy reaches across and pats my head.

'Dallas,' he says.

'What?'

'Are you all right, Dallas?'

I think about being all right. It doesn't mean the same thing as it used to.

'Yes,' I say. 'Go to sleep, it's the middle of the night.'

8

'How did your meeting go?' Mr Chaplin asks me.

'Not very well, sir. We're planning to have a protest now.'

'Have you thought any more about what you could do here, because . . .'

I sigh. 'All right. I'll do the assembly.'

'Tomorrow?' Aiza says. 'Have you gone insane?'

'Probably,' I agree. 'I don't want to think about it. Your trainers are cool.'

Ruby strokes the laces. The laces are gold. 'Where did you get them?'

'Online,' Aiza says, off-hand. She doesn't show off about new stuff. Also, she doesn't seem to want to talk about the fact that she stole her father's phone and woke us up in the middle of Saturday night from somebody else's bathroom to fret about his love life. 'Dad's feeling guilty for being out so much, so he keeps buying me stuff. We're going to Ibiza in the summer too, he told me last night. On our own. I made that clear.'

'Ibiza?' Libby says. We're in the cloakroom and I didn't see her through a wall of Year 5s. 'You're going to Ibiza with your dad? What are you going to be doing, going to foam parties together?'

'No,' says Aiza. 'Ibiza's an island, genius. Full of nice beaches and stuff. Sunny. Hot. Where are you going, Bournemouth?'

I catch Ruby's eye and think, Bournemouth would be OK.

'That would be a step up for you, Ruby, wouldn't it – Bournemouth? I'm going to Croatia, actually,' says Libby. She gets these red spots on her cheekbones when they start going on at each other like this.

'Oh yeah? We were talking about that a couple of years ago,' says Aiza, 'but it was a bit cheap.'

'I'm speaking at assembly tomorrow,' I say at dinner.

'Great,' says Gemma. 'I wish I could help you but I've just got so much work I have to get done tonight. Eat your broccoli, Violet.'

'You're an idiot,' says Sam. 'You're going to get roasted. Here,' he scrapes half his pork chop on to Billy's plate.

'Wow, sweetie,' says Jessi. 'That's pretty cool. You want to come spend the night with me and I'll hear you practise?'

Gemma slings her plate into the sink. 'There's no way you've got room for her in that tent.'

'I'm not that large,' I say, insulted.

'It's a beautiful night,' Jessi says. 'Warm as toast, stars going to be like diamonds. Forecast is for clear. I thought we'd sleep out.'

Gemma looks at me. 'You've got school tomorrow.'

'I know,' I say. 'That's the point. I've got to *prepare*. And you said you had to work late anyway.'

Jessi makes a fire and we sit beside it. It's the blue side of the evening and the colour of the flames gets deeper and deeper as we sit. Jessi plays her guitar while I toast the s'mores. She sings Momma's favourite song, about the girl with the homespun disposition, who's as Texas as can be.

We talk about Momma. I like to talk about her now, sometimes, and even though I get that feeling in my nose like I might cry, it's not horrible. We talk about Sam, and Billy, and about Granma living over in Texas on the farm.

Jessi asks me about boys, and I squirm and shake my head, though I can picture that one day, when I've got something to tell, I might be able to tell it to her. It's not till later, till we're curled up in sleeping bags with our toes near the fire and our pillows further away so we can look at the stars – Jessi only knows the Big Dipper and the Little Dipper, which makes me wonder where Momma got all the stuff she knew: 'Out of books most likely,' says Jessi, 'that was your momma's way' – that we talk about the future. The Future.

'How you doing, Dallas?' she asks.

'All right.'

'Is all right enough? Is it going to be enough? Dallas?'

I can smell nettles and water and hear frogs and birds and

feel the grass under my palms, but when you stay still on your back awhile in this meadow it can feel like there's nothing at all but sky, nothing between you and gazillions of stars, like you could just fall away from the Earth and into that silver and black. 'What?'

'You want to come back to Texas with me?'

My heart drops back into my body with a thump. 'For a holiday?'

'No,' she says. 'Dallas, you're not happy at home. OK, it's nobody's fault because you all are still dealing with the loss, and Gemma's crazy busy, and Sam – who knows what's going on with Sam and bless his heart – but Dallas, you deserve to have some space *and* you deserve to be looked after. You deserve to be first on somebody's list.' She takes my hand. 'You're first on my list.'

It's exciting, and scary, thinking about it – not being here any more. Being somewhere else instead. She says I'd love Texas. I know I love Texas. I think about Billy and Sam but it's too weird. She says I'd love to live in Austin, it's the coolest city in the world, and the whole state lying around it with all the space and my bones belong there and there's nothing I couldn't grow up to be.

'I couldn't be president,' I point out.

'Why not?' she says, annoyed.

'I was born in England.'

'So you grow up and get the rules changed.'

'You want me to change the American Constitution?'

'Yes, Dallas, goddammit. If that's what you want.'

She says she's been looking for a reason to settle down all her life, and most especially the last couple of years, and can't I just imagine it, the two of us sharing a little house with a big yard and maybe a cat or even a dog and it would be just exactly what she and my momma planned years ago when they were teenagers but never got to do, and how peaceful it would be and I could bring my friends home?

Too many thoughts. Bringing friends home and it's not Aiza and Ruby. A little house in Austin with a dog. Billy. Sam. What it will be like to be here, after summer, with Sam gone. Or Sam different, because if he does stay here he will be different – if he gives up on going to uni. In a different school, huge, without Ruby or Aiza in my class anyway. And no library.

I think about Billy being here with no Sam and no library and no me. Though when Momma told us about my dad leaving, she said nobody ought to stay where they are just out of guilt . . .

'What do you think I'm doing here?' Jessi demands. 'Spending all my savings so I can pass my days in an English meadow? I'm here to bring you back home with me, sweetie, where you belong.'

She says she'll never have a daughter of her own now but I'm as precious to her as a daughter could ever be and maybe more because I'm the closest thing to my momma left in this world and my momma was the human being she loved the most.

The thing is, Jessi is the closest thing to Momma for me as well.

We forget to prepare for the assembly.

'So,' I say to the WHOLE SCHOOL except Early Years, and I never knew before how many pairs of eyes there were in the school, or how many smirking mouths – I look back down quickly – 'the council are going to shut down Queen Street library and I think that's really bad and I was wondering if some of you would like to help campaign against it.'

I'm doing this badly. It's no surprise, but I was hoping that I cared about it enough to be suddenly brilliant at speaking in front of an audience. No. I need to make them interested. Sam said I should say that they're going to shut down our access to the future unless we all get out and protest. I'm not sure if he believes it himself, and anyway I've cocked it up now. I chance another look up, and unfortunately happen to see Gilbert Finch with his tongue sticking out. He has this long tongue.

'I just want to read you a couple of things about libraries,' I say, 'which the teachers thought would be a good idea.'

It's unusual, how little control over my mouth my brain has right now.

I read them some paragraphs. Too fast, but they look so bored, I just want this to be over. I read them a bit about the library from *Harry Potter*, with the screechy books and terrifying librarian, and remind them about the one in *Doctor Who*. There's a Terry Pratchett bit that Gemma forced into my hands this morning. Not even a titter. Some sniggering when I drop two of my pages on the floor. One of them slides away and I have to chase it – it ends up under the altar and Rev Flinders fishes it out for me.

'So,' I say, going back to the microphone even though in many ways I'd rather die, 'libraries are important and Queen Street library is important and if you think at all, in any way, that it's important, please do come and speak to me – and we're going to have a protest at the library next Saturday afternoon, not this one coming but next Saturday, at two o'clock. So if you could come, that would be awesome.'

Then I try to go to the back of the hall where the rest of my class are, even though Libby is openly laughing at me and Gilbert Finch is doing something weird with his head, but I can't get through the teachers and the piled-up Year 4s who came in late and didn't spread out properly, so I duck into the corridor and sit on the windowsill and breathe. Mr Chaplin looks out at me but he doesn't make me come back in. The headteacher, Ms O'Leary, is talking about me and how I'm brave and how they should support me. I press one of my ears up against the window and think about the holidays. They're going to be long, this year – whether I'm here or in Texas . . .

* * *

'I asked my dad about my mum,' Aiza says, out of the blue.

Ruby looks up from where she's balancing along the churchyard wall. 'How come?'

'I don't know.' She shrugs. 'I was pretending to be sad about her so that he'd feel sorry for me and ditch this *woman*.'

'You're rotten,' I say. 'What did he say?'

She shrugs again. 'He says he doesn't know where she is, hasn't heard from her in years. But . . . he says he reckons she's not dead.'

I lean back and stare at the sky, so as not to see them look at me out of the corners of their eyes.

'Did you think she was?'

'No.'

I consider Aiza, all these years, wondering if her mother was dead.

'I mean, I used to think she probably was. It was nicer, in a way. I know that sounds cold, but I used to picture her looking down on me, or whatever. From up there.' Aiza waves her strawberry split at the sky. 'I don't think that any more,' she adds quickly, 'that it would be nicer. It's just – never knowing her . . .'

I try to say with my body language that it's OK, because I don't know how to in words, and she relaxes.

'Do you believe all of that?' Ruby asks her. 'About heaven?'

'I'm a Muslim, Rubes, it's a well-developed religion and everything. We're not completely lacking in, like, the concept of an afterlife.'

Ruby nods as if that's interesting and munches her Fab.

We're sitting on the fence outside St Luke's church. It sits on the canal and you would think you were in the countryside – it's old and golden with a tower and everything. There must have been a wedding today; there are mashed rose petals all over the path.

'It'd be nice getting married here,' I say.

Aiza licks melty red and white stuff off her wrist. 'You could.'

'I don't know if I could,' I say, 'it's a Protestant church, and I'm Catholic.'

'Well, if they wouldn't have you they definitely wouldn't have me.'

The wall we're sitting on is probably about two hundred years old or something. On a day like today, sitting in the shade looking at the sun, you can't help but let the trouble drain out of you. Just a bit. If you don't think too hard.

'It's weird,' says Aiza.

'What?'

'I don't know – old buildings like that, I suppose. I mean, we've got enough of them in Oxford. My cousin in Leeds can't stop taking pictures whenever she's down here, she says she could use them to start a postcard business.'

'I don't know,' I say. 'I guess sometimes you think about history and stuff.'

Aiza lobs her stick behind a green gravestone that doesn't look like it ever had anything written on it. I suppose it's biodegradable. 'But do you feel like you own it? I look at it and sometimes it's like you get a thrill, because it's history, like you say, and you feel all connected with it or whatever.'

I sort of know what she means. Once Momma took us to the Tower of London and we stood right where Anne Boleyn got her head chopped off and I felt weird. Because it happened just right there, right where I was, and for a second I got a flash of it and it was unsettling.

'And then,' Aiza says, 'I think, but six hundred years ago, Aiza, you weren't rocking it round Oxford.'

'Well,' Ruby says, 'yeah.'

'You know what I mean though. My ancestors or whatever weren't here, they weren't in green old England, they were in Pakistan. Only it wasn't even Pakistan, I don't even know what it was.' She sucks her knuckle.

'You could find out,' I say.

'Yeah, I know.'

'Mine weren't either,' I say, looking up at the tower. 'Half of mine were hopping round Scotland under a grey sky, and the other lot were in Texas. Well, not six hundred years ago, I suppose.'

'Why not?' says Ruby.

'It didn't exist,' I explain. 'The Europeans hadn't pinched America then. I'd have had some in Mexico I think, and the rest were still in Spain. And Germany.'

'You're a right hotchpotch, aren't you, Dallas,' Aiza says.

We all look up at the church.

113

'What about you, Rubes?' asks Aiza. 'Your mum's from round here, isn't she?'

'Yeah,' says Ruby. 'Bridge Street. And my dad. They lived opposite each other.'

'Anyone from anywhere else?' Aiza asks.

'I don't think so. Both my grans are from Oxford.'

We contemplate Ruby's ancestors, long-ago Coxes with freckles and scraped elbows, probably wading over the Thames with a herd of oxen.

'Well,' I say, 'it can be you then, you can get married here and we'll be your bridesmaids.'

'I don't think I'll get married,' says Ruby. 'Are we doing these leaflets or what?'

'We got off the point,' Aiza says. We've done one street and now we're trudging round the corner to the second. It's getting on for five o'clock but it's still boiling. I wish we hadn't already eaten our ice lollies.

'What point?'

'Me.'

'Oh. Of course,' I say.

'Do you realise what could happen, if my dad is serious about this – creature?'

'She might come and live with you,' nods Ruby.

'Maybe they'll get married,' I suggest.

'They might have babies,' Ruby ponders.

'Unbelievable,' says Aiza. She's stopped, plumb in the

middle of the road we're crossing. Dramatic as ever. I pull her on to the pavement as a car toots. 'You two are unbelievable. I hate my friends. Are we doing this or what?' She trots up to the first door and shoves a leaflet through the letterbox. 'This is so pathetic, Dallas. You owe me so much right now.'

'I think it's cool.' Ruby beams. A dog barks right behind the front door she's standing at, and she drops her whole pile of leaflets all over the path and flower bed. By the time she's picked them up Aiza and I are halfway down the road. The novelty is wearing off quickly.

'Do you think anyone will come?' Ruby asks, catching us up. She's looking at a leaflet. I think they're pretty good, Aiza drew ninjas all over them and Jessi helped me get the words more brash – and then Gemma made them more English and Sam put in the punctuation. 'If you care about libraries,' she reads out, slowly, 'or if you think everyone, not just wealthy people, should have the right to read books and access information, then get your voice heard.'

'I can't see anyone actually turning up,' says Aiza.

'Oh brilliant,' I say.

'Well, you've got to be realistic, Dallas. Nobody's ever even in Queen Street library. Why would they show up on a Saturday to save it?'

I'm so distracted thinking about this that I accidentally push a leaflet through the front door I'm standing at, even though it has a *NO LEAFLETS* sticker at the side. Before

I get back to the street, the door flies open, and this man appears, kicks the leaflet at me and shouts, 'TAKE THE BLOODY THING AWAY!'

I drop my pile of leaflets.

Quicker than I can think, Aiza is at one side of me and Ruby is at the other. 'Get stuffed, you massive git,' Ruby yells, chucking a screwed-up leaflet at him, while Aiza's shouting, 'What's wrong with you, speaking to defenceless little girls like that, you huge turd?'

A couple of other doors open, and the man shuts his pretty quickly.

9

I think everybody's forgotten about my assembly, which probably makes the whole thing totally pointless but still, let's not pretend it isn't a relief. We've got another post-SATs, the-teacher's-given-up trip today, to Cluny's, which is this outrageously posh school not far away from ours. It has a huge meadow the length of a street and a river running at the bottom of it, plus basketball and tennis courts, and a swimming pool and a real theatre inside. It must be strange to actually go there.

It turns out they're all off on their holidays already, apart from a few who have stayed for 'summer school', whatever that is – the teacher who's telling us about it ('My name is Kezia Fairbright') makes out like it's ace. Maybe they ride horses or something. Anyway, they're nowhere near us. We're just there, along with Year 6s from St Matthew's and some other grubby primary schools like ours, to learn archery and mad stuff like that.

'I wish we could just go back to school and do maths,' I say to Ruby.

'It'll be fine,' she tells me kindly.

'Everyone better get out of the way anyway when it's my turn. You know how good my aim is.'

'What's even wrong with you, Dallas?' says Libby's voice behind me. 'You'd rather be doing maths? You're such a weirdo.'

'Oh, shut up, Elizabeth,' I say.

'That's not my name.'

'Well, it should be.'

'Nerd.'

'Yeah, so I'm a nerd, so what? At least I don't have fantasies about waving bows and arrows round like some cartoon fox.'

'Oh my God, you're so weird.'

'Leave her alone,' Ruby says suddenly.

Libby laughs. So does Jada. 'Look who's getting stuck in. I don't think Dallas needs you to defend her. She is Mr Strong.'

Mr Strong is something Gilbert Finch used to call me a couple of years ago because he said I was square. It hurts my feelings and I shove her. Aiza, who's on the other side of our group, bouncing up and down waiting for her go, must spot that we're having an argument, because she suddenly pings an arrow over everyone's head, which almost falls right on Libby's head. Libby shrieks and stumbles over Paolo. I swear I don't know how Aiza does the stuff she does.

'Aiza,' Mr Chaplin says, 'don't do that again, yeah?'

'Little girl!' calls the Cluny teacher, Mrs Fairbright, in this severe voice. She stalks over to our class. 'Little girl, let me see you do that again and you will have to sit to one side for the rest of the morning.'

I see Aiza's lips moving, mouthing 'big deal'.

'These are not toys. We are treating you like responsible young men and women, allowing you to handle this equipment. Please do not make us regret that trust.' She stares at Aiza, who stares back. 'I think you had better go to the back of the line for now.'

Aiza stomps over to us, trying to kick Libby on the way, and Gilbert Finch fires an arrow precisely as Mrs Fairbright comes to tell him how to do it, just missing hitting her in the shoulder.

'This is tragic,' Aiza says, as we sit on the riverbank eating our sandwiches.

I look down at the river, swirling along. The current is always strong here, maybe because it's quite narrow. It's a good place to swim. There's a 'bathing point' not far from here that Momma used to take us to – it's funny. I never minded this field being for rich kids only when I was looking at it from in the river. It just looked pretty.

'Maybe we should swim away,' I say.

I would love to leave my lunchbox here, and most of my clothes, and just let myself fall into the water. Leave this day behind. My skin itches, thinking of it.

'Nah,' says Aiza, 'let's blow the place up instead. Tie dynamite to Kezia. Did you see her face when Gilbert Finch got his packet of beef jerky out?'

We've spent the morning queuing up to shoot arrows.

I couldn't even bend the bow at first, then the arrows just kept falling, and when I finally shot one it flew up in the air and hit the school, three floors up. I was standing with my back to the school. Mrs Fairbright said that, out of respect for the antique glazing, I'd better sit down now.

Later we're going to have a treasure hunt or a paper chase or something. 'I mean, they could at least let us in the swimming pool,' says Aiza.

'Or the theatre,' says Ruby wistfully.

We get up to wander back. If I move to Texas, I won't miss the way half of Oxford belongs to schools and colleges you're not meant to go into, but maybe I'll miss the way you can get around the edges of them without even trying hard. No one can kick you out of the river.

The river in Austin is the wild Colorado. Different.

Nobody from our class seems to be around when we get nearer to the school, except that as we stand near a flower bed so that Ruby can smell the roses, we hear Libby's voice behind the hedge that borders it.

'So are you like at the summer school or whatever?'

'Yeah,' says another voice, like something off *Made In Chelsea*, 'we, like, are.'

'What's it like?' Jada asks. 'The summer school?'

'It's OK. Aren't you supposed to be over there?'

By now, Aiza has carried over one end of the nearest bench, so I get the other, and we all clamber on and peep over the hedge. Libby and Jada are standing there talking to three girls a bit older than us who are literally wearing bikini tops and hot pants and lounging in deck chairs. 'I suppose this is home for them,' I whisper. Not that I wear a bikini top at home. Aiza frowns at me to shut up.

'We just came to have a look,' Libby says. 'What's it like, going here?'

'What's it like at your school?' asks the redheaded girl in the green top.

'Oh, you know. A bit rubbish. Full of freaks,' says Libby. 'I'm going to Headington Girls' in September.'

'Oh, are you?' says the redhead. 'We've just beaten them at tennis.'

'Do you ride horses?' asks Jada.

Aiza gets down from the bench and starts looking around in the flower beds.

'Shut up, Jada,' says Libby. 'Sorry about her. I like your shorts.'

'Thanks,' says the other girl, the one with long brown curls. 'I don't think much of yours.'

Libby forces a laugh, looking down at her navy shorts – we're all in PE kit. 'I know, they're embarrassing.'

I get down from the bench too, and take Aiza's arm to make her drop the twigs she's picking up to chuck over the hedge at them. I pull her round the corner to where the cricket pitch starts. I point at the sprinkler, which is peacefully greening up the wicket with a shower of beautiful, glistening water.

It's heavy, and we get fairly wet ourselves before Ruby

thinks of turning off the tap. Then Aiza and I pick it up and step back up on to the bench, trying not to grunt with the effort. I balance my end on my shoulder, and tip it carefully to get the angle right. I'm no good at pool or darts or crazy golf but I bet, if I try hard, I can aim a jet of water.

Aiza signals to Ruby, waiting by the tap.

The water flies out, nearly taking my ear off, and hits Libby smack in the middle of her back. Weaker jets take out Jada and the redheaded girl and the one with bobbed hair who looks like she just gets straight out of the shower looking like that. I've never heard screaming like it, and they're so confused that they can't even get out of the way, they just caper round with their eyes shut and their mouths open, falling over each other. I hear myself cackling like a witch, but I can't help it.

Then Mrs Fairbright comes belting round the corner of the building like a 100-metre runner, eyes blazing. Aiza shrieks and drops the sprinkler, which crashes about two metres down into the middle of the antique hedge but keeps spouting out water while I wrestle to get it back. I watch helplessly as the water hits Mrs Fairbright right in the chops and then continues to hit her. All over.

We drop the sprinkler, damaging the hedge a bit more, and duck frantically behind it, getting ourselves soaked. We look at each other. Behind us, Ruby turns the water off. Then we stand up slowly.

Mrs Fairbright has been waiting for us to appear. She

stands with her hands on her hips and her hair dripping into her eyes, looking at us. All the girls we shot are looking at us as well. I notice that we've accidentally aimed a whole lot of water at an open window and that the silky red curtains inside are soaking wet.

We get marched away to stand under a tree, and Mr Chaplin has to call school – our school – to get Miss Wheeler to come and help look after everyone while he marches us, and Libby and Jada, back to school. Our school.

Then Ms O'Leary lets us have it, over letting down ourselves, our class, Mr Chaplin, her, St John's, our parents, our country, the world – and we have to sit in Ms Wilson's office all afternoon twiddling our thumbs.

She calls our families too.

Ruby's mother actually arrives to pick her up at three o'clock. She's shirty with Ms Wilson, and when she takes Ruby's arm she nearly pulls her over. Aiza and I wave goodbye and then sit back down, both feeling rubbish. 'Poor old Ruby,' Aiza says.

Ms O'Leary comes back out of her office to give us one more go with her accusatory bright blue stare, and then tells us we can go.

When I get home – because I don't dare put it off by going round to Aiza's, and I don't want to listen to her dad yelling at her anyway – Gemma is livid. She even stops cleaning the sink to shout.

'I can't believe you would behave that stupidly,' she says, a few times.

'Come on,' says Jessi. 'It was water, not battery acid.'

Gemma ignores her. 'Don't you realise that that kind of thing gives you a reputation, Dallas? We don't live in some huge city where you'll never see those people again. All those kids from other schools will be at school with you in September, and now they think you're the idiotic naughty one.'

'Ah, leave her be,' says Jessi.

Then Sam comes in from the park with Billy and looks disgusted with me.

'So this is the new Dallas, then, yeah? This is the path you've chosen? So I guess you're a bully now.'

I feel too tired to listen to them shout. All they ever want to say to me is what I should be doing and how I'm not doing it right. So I say I have to go to the library.

10

The next couple of days at school, being in disgrace and stuff, are quite boring. We're not allowed out at break time, and Ms O'Leary calls us into her office again just to tell us how lucky we are to be allowed to take part in any activities at all, and at lunchtime we have to help Ms Wilson and Mr Elgin, the site manager, sort out the Lost Property boxes.

'Phooey, this stinks,' Aiza says, bending over one of the big bins. 'I can't believe they're making us do this without gloves. Oh good grief.' She holds a pair of shorts between finger and thumb. 'Am I really expected to – probe – this for a name tape?'

'Yes, you are, Aiza,' Ms Wilson says, hurrying past. 'And if you don't get on with it, you can do the Early Years bin instead.'

'At least they don't have BO,' Aiza says.

'Their bins are full of underwear,' Ms Wilson says. 'Nor are they all gifted wipers.'

We shriek.

'So be grateful and get on with it. Now, Dallas,' Ms Wilson says, 'how are the plans for your protest going?'

* * *

125

We look at pictures. Partly to get ideas for good slogans, but also because they're sort of spellbinding, when you start studying them – people marching along, so wrapped up in the same thing. Jessi calls Granma up in Texas and gets her to email all the photos of Momma and Jessi at rallies and vigils. Momma looks so fierce in some of them, even though her hair is in plaits and she's wearing a peace sign T-shirt.

Gemma stoops over the table. 'God, she looks young,' she says.

'Long time gone,' says Jessi, opening a bottle of beer.

I put the Dixie Chicks on the stereo. I have to wipe my eyes off quickly before I sit down again.

'I'm proud of you, Dallas,' Gemma says unexpectedly.

'We're all proud of her,' says Jessi. She fingers the pictures again. 'I still know a lot of those folks. Most of them have wound up in Austin. Boy, would they be excited to meet you, Dallas.'

Aiza texts on Sunday. *Only a week left Dallas I hope youre working hard*

A pause, then *I want a good placard*

'I guess I better tell Gemma, soon, about you coming back with me,' says Jessi, when I'm saying goodnight to her. 'It's going to affect her plans, and all.'

'Yeah,' I say.

She nudges my cheek with her knuckle. 'You ain't changed your mind?'

I didn't know I'd made it up in the first place, but I guess it's time to. So I think, so hard that pieces of my brain probably flake away. I think about what everyone will say. Sam will slaughter me. I don't know if Gemma will even allow it, but Jessi seems to think she will, and maybe it will be sort of a relief. Gemma is so busy that she always seems about to crack, and I'm not like Sam, I'm not actually useful.

OK. I admit to myself that they'll both mind. Of course they'll mind. Because they think of me as their responsibility, and they probably don't trust Jessi – but that's not the same as if they needed me. Me, Dallas. Even Billy – Billy will miss me. My stomach gnaws a bit, thinking of that. He will miss me. But Momma said that thing about not staying just for guilt.

The thing is. We're all trying to get over this enormous mountain of sadness or whatever. I'm the river that's pooled up at the bottom and can't raise itself or find a way through, so I'm not much use to the others. Gemma keeps on striding and striding upwards, trying to drag us all with her, but it's so hard and I don't think even she knows where the top is. Sam's gone right back in the other direction, all he wants to do is pretend we're back four years ago with Billy just a baby and Momma asleep upstairs.

And who knows what Jessi thinks she wants, but maybe she's the dynamite that will blast a big hole and I can go through it to the other side. Even if not, I would be somewhere else; things would all be different; even if I was uncomfortable at home in Austin I wouldn't have to look round and remember being comfortable once. And she wants me. She thinks I can help her.

So I guess that's the decision made.

Thursday is Billy and Violet's settle-in day at school. All the classes at St John's go up a year to meet their new teachers and stuff, and the Early Years' rooms fill up with three and four year olds. Sadly this means us Year 6s have to go to the secondary school for sports-related activity.

The class gets split into two, and Ruby is on the wrong side. I only catch a glimpse of her every now and again, but twice I see Libby and Jada picking on her. We don't even get to have lunch together.

'What have they been saying to you?' I ask when we're finally near each other, waiting to run our laps in the relay right at the end.

'Who?'

'You know who.'

She shakes her head. 'Nothing. Doesn't matter.'

I study her, briefly. She looks like she's shrunk. 'Tell me what they said.'

'No,' she says simply, and takes off running. I wipe my hands on my shorts again, but I still drop the baton.

We trail back to school at quarter to three, dehydrated and damp. My feet feel as big as my head. We have to squeeze past a queue of eager new parents peering through the bars of the gate to catch a glimpse of their babies. Ruby's pointing something out to me. I come out of my daze to see that it's Violet, crying, cornered against the climbing frame by some puffy yahoo of a child in a white shirt.

I yell, but she doesn't hear me. She tries to push away from him but he won't let her.

I thrust my bag into Aiza's hands and prepare to push through everyone so I can run round and get out to her. I don't need to. Billy comes skip-running across the playground with a ball in his hands and lamps the puffy boy on the head with it, knocking him on his can. He bawls and runs off to a teacher. Billy stands still by Violet and watches with interest as the teacher moves towards him.

I go straight home, for a change. I figure it's the least I can do for Billy, in case the teacher made a big deal out of it or anything. The lurch, the crumb in my chest, has gotten so it doesn't bother me as much, but today is bad, because I keep wishing Momma was here to stick up for Billy. It's too hot to cry, and my face is salty enough already.

Billy and Violet are both on the sofa like limp rags. Violet's pink ballerina skirt, which she must have finally chosen after I left this morning, is rucked up round her so that she looks like a peony that's fallen off its twig and she has one leg up on the arm of the sofa, not very elegant but I know how she feels.

'How did today go?' I ask them. Billy looks calm so presumably he didn't get pre-expelled.

'OK,' says Violet. 'I got a best friend.'

'Already?'

'Yes, she's called Bea.'

'That's nice.' Poor kid. 'What about you, Billy, did you like school?'

'Nooo,' says Billy, tolerantly moving on the sofa so he can see the laptop past my legs.

I don't want to go anywhere near Gemma or Sam, but I need a drink. Sam is sitting at the far end of the kitchen table and Gemma is standing by the oven. They both go completely silent as I walk over and turn on the tap. You have to let it run for a minute or so before it's cold.

'I'm back,' I say brightly, getting out a glass.

Gemma coughs. 'How was your day?'

'Sporty. Awful.'

'Ah.'

Then they get back to having what Momma would have called a 'spirited discussion' about whether it was helpful for Sam to get shirty with Ms O'Leary over the kind of expectations teachers should have for Billy, and which of them was the first to suggest that Billy and Violet should be in different classes . . .

'On a day when they're getting their first impression of Billy, you go and make out like you don't want your own daughter to be exposed to him, like he's going to be a drag on the class.'

'And you told her that Violet is spoilt.'

'She is spoilt.'

Gemma throws her spatula across the room. 'That child is four years old and has been through hell for the last year. I am not comparing her loss to yours, or to Billy's, but still, one of the most important people in her life died and she's doing the best she can.'

Sam more or less storms off.

'I was proud of him,' Gemma says after a minute.

'Billy?'

'No, Sam. And yes of course Billy.'

'Why?'

'Well, he could have sounded less confrontational – but anyway he left Ms O'Leary in no doubt about how we feel about accepting Billy's autistic – not trying to fix him.'

Jessi is outside the back door, smoking. She raises her eyes to heaven.

'Why are you pulling that face, Jessi?' Gemma asks her. She's had a glass of wine or two.

'No face,' says Jessi.

'You rolled your eyes.'

'I may have *raised* my eyes.'

'Well, why did you raise your eyes?'

Jessi flicks her ash into the wisteria. 'I'm just enjoying the brainwashing job my sister, Lord love her, did on her kids.'

'You think Billy needs fixing?'

'Billy is the most adorable child I ever saw. And I worry over how the world's going to treat him.'

'I'm sure we all worry over that,' Gemma says. 'But Billy's just the way he ought to be. Let the world change.'

I go out to the bathroom to report this conversation to Sam. I suppose I'm hoping it might fix things between him and Gemma, take the wind out of his sails, but there's always more wind in my brother's sails than I could possibly do anything about.

'Good,' he says, rinsing the melted soap out of the soap dish. 'We still need her.'

'What do you mean, still?' He doesn't answer. He looks upset, I notice. Billy singing about five little ducks going quack quack quack – he can't make 'c' sounds so it sounds a bit rude – doesn't make him smile. He's also looking scruffy. 'Aren't you going out with Prue tonight?' They normally go out on Thursday nights, to some music pub quiz across town.

'No,' he says. Reaches for the towel.

'How come?'

He lifts Billy up and out of the water. 'Prue and I aren't together. Any more.'

I'm aghast. Prue's been around a long time, and for all the worst time. I thought she loved him.

'Why?'

He's drying Billy as thoroughly as he ever does, maybe more thoroughly, while Billy leans over his shoulder and drums on his back. 'We split up at the stupid prom. Look, Prue wants to go travelling, she wants to do all the usual things, she wants to go to Thailand and Vietnam and Cambodia and then she wants to go to Newcastle and have a great time and get a brilliant degree and have a life. What am I going to do, sit at home waiting for her to come back and break up with me?'

I follow him and Billy up to their bedroom, where Billy's PJs are already laid out on the bed. 'Do you want to talk about it?'

'What, with you?'

I feel myself get angry. I mean, I like Prue too. Not as much as he does, obviously, but people can't just disappear other people from your life and not even explain properly. 'Well, you probably should talk to someone.'

'Yeah, Dallas, because you're such a big talker through of things, aren't you? It took you eight months and Jessi being here before you'd even mention Momma's name. And even now you're hiding from it all with this ludicrous library thing, like you've got a chance in hell of making a difference. It's time you grew up.' He shuts the door in my face.

I go to my room. After a while Billy comes up to tell me dinner's ready. I'm crying, and when he notices he comes over and puts his arms round my neck, wiggling comfortably on to my lap. He stays there until I've more or less stopped, and then leads me by the hand to the top of the ladder.

Billy doesn't really need me, I know that. Sam has most things covered and Gemma's there for the rest. But he's lost enough, and if I'm going to leave him, I'm going to do the best I can to save other things he loves for him. *I'm* not going to leave a mess behind me when I go.

On the way to school I stop and knock on the library door. Gracie is already in there, setting up for the day. She lets me in and leaves me alone. I sit down on the floor by the picture books with the red D cushion and flick through, remembering lots that I used to love. Some of them are still the same editions, I can tell by the marks on the pages. There hasn't been any proper money going into this library for ages.

Then I get up and go over to the 9-12 shelves and pick off a book I've only read once before. *The Mixed-Up Files Of Mrs Basil E Frankweiler.* I read it years ago and I don't remember much about it except that it's about running away, but it was funny. Funny is good.

'I need to see Ms O'Leary,' I say as I'm handing over my phone.

Ms Wilson looks up at me. 'Do you?'

'Yes.' I watch Libby's back leave the office. No point getting mocked more than necessary. 'I want to say something in assembly,' I hiss.

'Well, I'm sure that will be fine,' Ms Wilson says. 'I'll tell her.'

* * *

I stand up.

Momma's advice again. Fake it through until you make it true. Be someone else. I can be an activist for five minutes.

'Yes, it's me again – get over it,' I say, because they're already shifting about getting ready to laugh. 'Listen. They're trying to shut down our library, Queen Street library, which is a place where everybody can go to read, borrow books, do research and find things out, use computers. I know for a lot of us that's stuff we can do at home – if you can hop on a computer in your bedroom, why should you care about a library having one you can use, right? If you don't like reading, or your parents buy you new books every week, why should you care about a library having books that anyone can borrow?

'But the thing is,' I say, 'not everyone has that. There are people in this hall, and people living near Queen Street, who don't have computers at home, who don't have books at home, maybe because they don't have the space to keep them, or they don't have the money to buy them, or they don't have a home at all. I know a homeless man who's nice and a good man and he loves the library because they don't kick him out after half an hour if he can't afford another cup of tea, and he can read books there, or the newspaper. I've seen families taking their kids there because they've got loads of books in other languages that they don't sell in Waterstones. My brother's used it all his life to do his homework because we don't have any quiet at home, and that's why he's kept passing exams. If these people hadn't had the library, they wouldn't have had those things – we're talking about people's futures as well as their presents.

'And your futures too – even if you don't use it now, you might one day,' I shout at them, wiping my hands on my T-shirt. 'The council want to sell it to someone who's going to build fancy posh flats, as if we don't have enough of those already. That's not going to do anyone any good except rich people who'll get a bit richer off it. Once the library has gone, it's gone. That's your right to read, there. If something happens so you can't buy all the books you want any more – well, you won't be able to get them at all. You won't be able to go there and ask a trained librarian for help looking up information. You won't have a warm dry room full of books you can sit in any old day, on Queen Street. They'll have taken that away from you and sold it. Is that OK by you?'

I'm not expecting a response, but I get one. Aiza scrambles to her feet to shout 'NO!' but a few other people shout it too. My heart is thudding.

'If it's not, there's an easy thing you can do to try to stop it. There's a march tomorrow, from the library to the council. It's not far. Come along to the library, Queen Street library, at two o'clock, and join in. The more of us there are, the more likely we are to win.'

'Ask your mothers first!' Ms O'Leary shouts, getting up behind me.

'Bring them!' I call. 'Bring your mothers!'

* * *

136

'Well,' says Aiza afterwards.

'You were brilliant, Dallas,' says Ruby.

'Nice speech, Dallas,' Libby sneers at me at lunchtime. 'Not boring at all.'

'You've got doughnut on your chin,' Ruby tells her.

11

By Saturday afternoon we're ready.

Gemma and Jessi have both told me I don't have to do anything beyond read the words we've all written. It's just going to be people who have gathered outside the library, marching up Queen Street, along the main road and up to the council – only about a half-mile walk. It's not a big deal, except if it works.

I plait my hair and put on a grey T-shirt and shorts. I shouldn't wear anything distracting, Jessi says, in case there are pictures taken, not that it stops her wearing a skirt so short you could hardly blow your nose on it. She has plaits too. Sam asks if it's necessary for us to look like something out of *The Sound Of Music*. Billy is holding a tiny placard that says *I LIKE BOOKS BETTER THAN LUXURY FLATS*, and Sam can't help laughing when he looks at him, but he still refuses to come.

Gemma's just in jeans like she always is at weekends, but she's wearing Momma's favourite top, which is blue and edged with sequins. And Violet, in her green fairy outfit, is carrying a heart-shaped placard that reads *WHEN I NEED TO LEARN ABOUT SOMETHING I LOOK IN A BOOK.*

'Not exactly pithy,' comments Jessi. She takes off her jacket to reveal a white vest with *STOP LOOKING AT MY BOOKS* written across her chest. The K on '*BOOKS*' looks very much like a B.

'Classy,' says Sam.

So I suppose I thought I would be there with my plaits surrounded by people all striving for the same thing, and that the whole experience would have singing, and chanting, and laughter, and righteous anger or whatever. Like Jessi's pictures.

But in actual fact when we get there, there isn't a crowd of like-minded people. There's us, my family, and there's Gracie, naturally, and Danny and Annie from the boats, and Roger and another homeless man, and three women with children younger than me who've brought their own placards and don't seem to speak much English, and Aiza and Ruby who look embarrassed, and another librarian that Gracie knows, and Ms Wilson from school. And a reporter who's got a camera hanging round her neck.

That's it.

At least, Gemma says, the reporter seems to be on our side. She's trying to crush us together in a tiny space outside the library so it will look like there's more of us. 'It'll look good,' she keeps saying, dancing round us with her camera.

'Never mind,' Gemma says, looking down at me. 'It's not the numbers that matter.'

'Hell no,' says Jessi, jumping up and down. 'It's the spirit. It's the passion. It's the noise!' She throws back her head and whoops.

Aiza opens a bag of Skittles and passes it to me. 'So this sucks, right?'

'I think it's fun,' says Ruby, rummaging in the bag. 'Your auntie's well weird, Dallas.'

My phone beeps and I sneak a look at it. Sam's text says *Remember the Alamo*. I grin. Sometimes you get people's sympathy more when you look a bit pathetic and your numbers are tiny.

'We should get moving,' Gemma says.

And then there's a shout from the top of the street and we look up. And what looks like an army of people come marching down towards us.

'Oh my,' says Jessi.

I can see half my class and some from the other Year 6 class, and Mr Chaplin is there with four of his own children, and I see some Year 5 girls, and some Year 3 boys, and a host of even littler ones, and Ms O'Leary carrying a tin whistle.

'Dallas,' says Gemma. 'What did you do?'

People swirl around, clapping me on the back. I read out the speech we wrote, trying to look up every now and then, but nearly all these people have already heard me and my ten-gallon mouth talking about the library. Thank goodness we set off almost immediately.

The reporter clambers down off her car bonnet, where she

was taking pictures, and runs round us in circles trying to get the best angle. Unfortunately, it's like Sam said: she thinks I'm the story. She walks beside me most of the way to the council buildings, asking me questions.

'Why does it mean so much to you?'

I call up the speech I made in assembly. I try to shout less.

'But why does it mean so much to *you*?'

I tell her that I live in a house that's tiny and doesn't have room for bookshelves but that I love reading. I tell her it's the same for people like Gracie, and our other friends who live on the boats – that we don't have the space to keep books but we still need them. I tell her about Roger, and I try to get Roger to tell her himself but he isn't into it. I tell her about Sam studying there when we had two toddlers yelling all the time at home.

The reporter keeps looking at me. 'Any special memories of this library?' she asks.

My throat closes up. Aiza and Ruby are walking so close behind me, giggling, that when I slow up for a second Ruby treads on the back of my shoe and pulls it off.

'Oops,' she says. 'Sorry, Dallas.'

Then they move around me and start talking to Ms Wilson, and it's just me and the reporter at the back. So I tell her some stuff, and she keeps making her notes. Then because she asks, I tell her something about Momma too, and books, and how she brought us up to think that you have to stand up for stuff.

Then, thank God, we get to the council buildings, and after taking a couple more pictures she goes away, inside – she says she's going to try to find somebody on their side to talk to. 'If they're not all relaxing on their yachts,' Jessi mutters. Some people look at us out of the windows, and a policeman in a yellow jacket tells the adults not to block the pavement, and a couple of cars toot at us, and then we go home.

'Sounds like you got more people than I thought you would,' Sam remarks. 'You'd have needed hundreds though, to make any difference. Still an utter waste of time.'

'Thank you, Sam,' Gemma says. 'I thought it went well.'

Jessi waves a hand. 'We won't know how it went till we see the papers.'

'I'm exhausted,' says Gemma. 'Let's get fish and chips.'

'Yeah!' says Billy.

'Can I have chicken instead?' says Violet.

'We must be the most lard-ridden family in this city,' says Sam.

'Great idea, Gemma,' says Jessi. 'Give yourself the night off.'

'Well boring,' is what Aiza says about it. 'I thought it would be all firecrackers and chanting and people chucking bottles at us.'

'Sorry,' I say. 'Next time we'll be sure to incite a riot.'

It's windy today, a hot wind and raggy white clouds whizzing by above us. We've walked way up the towpath. It's funny, the centre of town is bum to belt buckle with tourists all summer, but hardly any of them bother to go anywhere on the river except the pubs. We're heading for our favourite swimming place, where you never see anyone except people walking their dogs and they don't care – because we're not actually supposed to swim in the river, not without an adult. But we always do. And if the grown-ups are going to argue all the time they can't expect me to stay at home.

'My nan's dog died last night,' says Ruby. 'Trudie.'

Neither of us knows what to say. It's not like a person dying, you don't know how upset somebody's going to be about a pet.

'Oh well,' Aiza says in the end, 'it's probably better than if she'd been sick for ages. My cousin had a dog and it used to just poo everywhere and be smelly for years before it died.'

Ruby giggles. 'Yeah, thanks.'

'No problem.'

'I expect she's in doggy paradise now,' I contribute. 'Cats with three legs to chase, and slow rabbits.'

'Balls flying around in the air by themselves,' Aiza agrees.

'Do you believe in that?' Ruby asks her.

'What, flying balls? Oh, doggy paradise?'

'Yeah.'

'I don't know. Why do you keep asking me what I believe?'

Aiza dips her feet in the river. 'Oof, that's cold. What do you believe?'

'Not much,' Ruby says.

I eat a Jammie Dodger; Aiza brought them with her. She always brings food on walks. She says walking with no food is for old people. 'I mean, why would humans get heaven and not animals?' I say, brushing off the crumbs. 'Anyway, my granma says heaven would be no good to her without her horses.'

Aiza takes the biscuits off my lap. 'Yeah, but which one will be her favourite horse, in eternity?'

'What about the scarf thing?' Ruby interrupts. 'Are you going to wear one of those?'

'A hijab?'

'Yeah, a hijab.'

Aiza laughs. 'No, I don't think so. Probably not. Not – anyway –' she steps out of her shorts and kicks them further up the bank – 'while I'm still going round in a swimsuit out of doors.'

I step up on the highest part of the bank, gather myself together and leap into the air. There's always a quarter of a second where I seem to hang, and the water seems terrifying, just for that moment. Then I plunge in and it's friendly again. I wouldn't have asked Aiza myself, it's sort of an awkward kind of question, although maybe it shouldn't be if she's my best friend and everything. Anyway, I don't know if I've ever thought about it before. 'Your dad wouldn't want you to wear one?'

'Nah.' Aiza turns over on her back and floats. 'You know my dad. He's not like that.'

'He wanted to send you to a girls' school.' Ruby comes one step further. It always takes her a while to get in, she's skinny and she feels the cold more than us.

Aiza shrugs. It's true, for a while she was threatened with Headington Girls', but she says she was never scared, because she can talk her dad in or out of anything. 'It would be up to me.' She looks at Ruby for a few seconds, curiously. 'Would you mind if I started wearing one, Rubes?'

Ruby swims under the ferns, which grow out of the bank, and disturbs a duck, which flies off complaining about kids making a hubbub on a Sunday afternoon. 'I suppose not. Only it's a bit weird, isn't it.'

'Why is it weird?' Aiza asks.

'I don't know. Like, I don't get why you'd want to cover your hair.'

'Well, I can explain it to you if you want.' Aiza's getting snippy, and I can't blame her, but I also don't like people getting cross with Ruby. I let go of the bank and let the current swirl me into the middle. I like seeing where it takes me. It takes me to Ruby, so I kick her. Just a bit. 'I can see why you would wear one,' Aiza says. 'To tell everyone else to get stuffed. You're quiet, Dallas. What do you think about hijabs? Would you disown me if I started wearing one?'

I revolve slowly, just flapping my hands enough to stay afloat. I love the river. 'Of course I wouldn't. You clown.'

'But would you judge me? You'd think it was crap, wouldn't you?'

'I wouldn't think it was crap.'

'Like, anti-feminist and stuff. You can say what you think.'

'Aiza,' says Ruby.

'I'm asking Dallas, Rubes.'

'Aiza, you're about to get run down by a punt.'

'Bloody kids,' the man in the punt growls as he nearly puts his pole down on Aiza's head – even though she's swimming away as fast as she can. I mean, he's supposed to look where he's going as well. What if she'd been an injured swan or something?

'Or a blind mallard,' agrees Ruby.

'Oh shut up, you two,' Aiza says, shaking some weed off her shoulder. 'I'm sick of this stupid river. Let's go back to mine. Unless you're afraid you'll get radicalised, Ruby?'

'I don't even know what that means,' Ruby says.

We eat a load of crackers and cheese at Aiza's house, and watch *Whip It*. I've seen it before but the end makes me start crying today. I've got a cushion on my lap so I just move it around a bit and I don't think the other two notice.

'Any more news about your dad's girlfriend?' I ask, when I've recovered.

Aiza looks moody. 'No. Apparently she wants to come to my gymnastics grading.'

'What? Why?'

'Oh, because she used to be sooooo good at gymnastics herself. Like, she somersaulted for the county. So, obviously.'

On the way home I ask Ruby about why she keeps coming up with questions about religion for Aiza.

She kicks a beer can across the road. 'I was just wondering.'

'Yeah. It's sort of funny, isn't it, we don't talk about it that much. I suppose I don't know what she believes. Or what you do, or anything.'

'I don't believe in much,' says Ruby.

'Would a hijab bother you?' I ask. Not sure I want to hear the answer.

'I don't know. It would be like – she'd be different.'

'She'd still just be Aiza.'

Ruby doesn't say anything for a while. Then she says, 'My mum's boyfriend doesn't like Muslims.'

There doesn't seem to be much I can say to that. 'What boyfriend?'

'Paul.'

I think about Paul. He's been around for a while, I realise now.

'What do you mean, he doesn't like Muslims?'

'I mean, he says he doesn't. Like them.'

'What kind of a thing is that to say?'

'A racist thing,' Ruby says, shrugging.

'He sounds horrible.'

'I didn't think he was horrible, but he says stuff like that.

He told Mum she should stop me going round to Aiza's. He said, doesn't she know about how they brainwash little white girls and stuff.'

I feel like I should put my arm round her or something, but she keeps moving, with her hands in her pockets like always. 'What did your mum say?'

'She said, they're not all like that. She said, Aiza's dad doesn't even have a beard.'

I consider this. It doesn't seem to be exactly the point, but at least Ruby can still be friends with Aiza. I say so.

'Yeah,' says Ruby. She looks at me sideways. 'I don't think Mum's like that, really, you know. She just – she's not very good at arguing with men.'

There's nothing I can think of that will make Ruby feel better. I don't understand it enough. There's one thing you could say for Momma, she definitely had no trouble arguing with men.

I ask her if she wants to come back to mine for dinner and that makes her look a bit happier, so maybe I'm better at this than I think.

Gemma and Jessi both make a big fuss of Ruby, which is nice. Gemma's made roast chicken and even Sam bites his lip and doesn't criticise. There's loads of Yorkshire puddings so Billy is happy, and Ruby looks more than content. There's even apple pie for pudding, and custard. You would think we were a civilised family.

Then Jessi absolutely insists on doing the dishes, and Gemma won't leave her alone, although to be fair to Gemma it's hard to leave someone alone in our house, which is basically all one room downstairs. Sam has gone out to get drunk with some of his friends and Billy and Violet are playing together for once, at Connect 4. Gemma picks up his guitar and starts singing 'Violet' by Frank Black. Violet looks pleased, but doesn't let it stop her beating Billy.

Jessi swooshes the last wet plate on to the rack and puts 'Billy Austin' by Steve Earle on the stereo.

'Right,' says Gemma. 'I guess I'll pack the guitar away then.'

Jessi comes with me to walk Ruby home.

'You're back at your mum's?' I ask, as Ruby turns right along the towpath.

'Yeah,' she says. 'She said I had to.'

After she's waved goodbye and got into the lift, I go outside, where Jessi is standing looking at the moon above the river. The water is wide and shallow here and the reflection isn't a nice neat moon-shaped one, it's a wild patch of shifting gold.

'Poor old Ruby, eh,' she says, turning round to me. I don't ask why. Ruby just is poor old Ruby. 'You know, it's tough all over.'

'Yeah,' I say.

'Everywhere you go, there's people having times . . .'

'Yeah.'

'And everywhere you go – you know – there's people to help out.'

I turn my head to look at her, but all I can see is the glowing end of her cigarette. 'I suppose so.'

She laughs. The cigarette end goes flying out of her mouth and disappears – I hear her grinding it with her foot. 'You sound so English sometimes. "I suppose so." My God, do you think I ever reckoned on a niece who talked like you?'

I flinch, a little bit, since it's dark. 'I guess you didn't.'

She puts her arm round me. 'Honey, you can't help that. That's all down to your Momma, God rest her. No. You're doing the best you can, all ways. And when I get you back to Texas – folks are going to go wild over you and your crazy English accent.'

12

I check the website of the local paper. There's nothing about the march.

'She said it might not be in today,' says Gemma.

'Hey, Dallas,' shouts Libby as I come into the classroom. 'How'd your tragic protest go?'

'Yeah,' says Jada, 'are you going to do another assembly?'

'Oh yes, please,' says Libby, 'do another assembly and tell us about it.'

'Shut your face,' says Ruby, who seems to have lost the ability to ignore them.

'What's up, Ruby, were you there too?'

'Yeah, Ruby, what were you doing there? I wouldn't have thought libraries were your thing. Thought you had to actually be able to read.'

Aiza takes Libby's fancy red school bag off her peg, holds it out so Libby looks, then licks it, right along the metal clip and over the catch. The boys howl. Gilbert Finch flicks a big white rubber at Jada's head.

* * *

Nothing on the website today either.

Jessi's come to the newsagent's with me this morning, and she makes me go in. She's wearing her STOP LOOKING AT MY BOOKS vest again, which the man behind the counter seems amused about, but Jessi ignores him, flipping through the paper from back to front and then from front to back, just to make sure.

'It's not there,' I say. 'That's last week's anyway. The print version doesn't come out till tomorrow.'

'I see that. Listen, don't fret yourself. It'll be in then.'

'Yeah,' I say, plunging back out through the door into the sunshine. Sam says nobody reads it anyway, he says we could get the front-page headline and nobody would give a stuff. I just feel like everything is tailing off and I'm not doing anything properly.

Jessi follows me out, lighting a cigarette and waving the paper around.

'What did you buy it for?' I ask.

'Your favourite auntie has had the hell of an idea.'

'What?'

'You know how I can't stand to see your face like this. Look at you. Like the cheese fell off your cracker. So I been thinking, what can I do to cheer Dallas up?'

'Yeah?'

'And then I seen this.' She flaps the paper open, pins it to the wall with her elbow and points.

'What?' I just want to get to school now, or I don't but

I might as well, but I look. It's the advert page. A bunch of concerts advertised, names I don't know, including the one Jessi has her thumb planted on. Well, Joe Dillon sounds vaguely familiar, I suppose.

'I don't know who that is,' I say.

'Whaaaaat?'

'I don't.'

'Not know Joe Dillon? The greatest living Texan singer after Willie Nelson?'

'No he isn't,' I say, because Steve Earle and Beyoncé, just off the top of my head.

'Well. Top ten anyway. Your momma liked him.'

'Did she?' I look more closely. 'Would I be allowed? Do you mean the Birmingham gig?'

'No, that's not till Friday. We don't have that kind of time to waste, not when Dallas's spirits are low.' She pinches my cheek. 'He's in London tonight.'

'Tonight's a school night,' I point out, since it's not like that fact will escape Gemma.

She looks at me for a long moment. 'Kid, you've earned yourself some room this year.'

'Gemma . . .'

'Leave Gemma to me. What is it? Don't you want to go? I thought you loved music.'

'Yeah,' I say.

'Your momma and I used to sneak out when she was around your age – maybe a little older but not much, and drive up to Austin. Course we always got caught because the gas would be so low, after, but it was worth it to hang around the bars and see the greats playing – one time we hitched to Houston . . . You worried I'm going to embarrass you? How about if you had your friends along?'

'Really?'

'Sure. A trip for four to London, why not? Tell you what. I'll pick you up from school early and we'll go get you some gear so you look the part, what do you say?'

Not that it matters what I say. She hatches a plan where she picks me up at lunchtime and we go shopping and then pick up Ruby and Aiza at three o'clock and all go to London. She says she's going to sort it out with Aiza's dad and Ruby's mum. I don't believe any of it will happen, but I agree to hang around the office at one o'clock and go into school feeling sort of agreeably interested, like it might not just be another day of watching people have arguments everywhere and sometimes getting drawn into them.

'Trust me,' she yells after me. I turn around to see her sauntering off in her denim shorts and white vest, and all the dads watching her go.

'Who?' says Aiza.

'Joe Dillon,' I say. 'I think he's, like, a fairly old rock star.'

'How old?'

'Probably fifty or something?'

She screws up her face. Ruby leans back against me,

concentrating; she's plaiting a piece of Aiza's hair. 'I've never been to a concert,' she says.

Aiza groans. 'So now I suppose we have to go.'

'You'll love it,' I say.

Jessi does turn up at one. I'm loitering near the office and I hear her telling Ms Wilson I have a dentist's appointment. Even though she's my aunt, which is practically my closest grown-up actual relative, it feels naughty skipping out of school with her two hours early.

'Oh,' I say when we get to the corner, 'I left my phone in Ms Wilson's drawer.'

'You won't need it,' she says, 'and we have to hustle. We got some stuff to buy.'

She says she's sorted it with everyone, and we're set to fetch Aiza and Ruby from school and be out all evening. I don't know when everybody got so permissive. Jessi takes me to Topshop and buys me a denim skirt. Even in the petite section all the tops are too big, so she says we'll go to H&M for a T-shirt. She literally buys coloured hairspray in the tattoo shop so that she can spray our hair on the train. None of this has ever happened to me before. She even buys bangles for all of us, and lip gloss in three different colours. I wonder if this is what it's going to be like, living with Jessi – a big sparkly haze of girliness.

'You all need to cut loose,' she says when I look surprised, and drags me into H&M where she slings ripped T-shirts in black, purple and pink over her arm and then picks out a strapless red top for herself.

'Your aunt's cool,' says Ruby when she comes back from the train toilet, wearing her purple T-shirt and with her sprayed hair tied up high in two pigtails – one silver, one pink and her usual blonde in between. 'Your turn, Aiza. This is so cool. I can't believe we're going to London on a Tuesday!'

Aiza snorts as she gets up and grabs the hairspray. 'Obviously my dad must have had plans with his – woman. He was probably thrilled.'

I go last, because I'm a coward and I didn't want to be sitting by myself with weird hair waiting for the others. The mirror is pathetic but I can still see enough to be startled. I often fantasise about looking completely different all of a sudden but now it's sort of happened for an evening it's weird. I mean I still look eleven. But suddenly I look like the kind of eleven-year-old who dresses up, who would wear a black T-shirt and a denim skirt – I never wear skirts. And my hair – it isn't brown. It's weird. I don't look as much like Sam as usual. I look like one day I might actually look like a girl.

'Wow,' says Aiza when I get back to our squished-up train table. She and Ruby are playing cards with a dirty old pack that Jessi pulled out of her bag.

'What?'

'You look like a girl.'

'We all do,' says Ruby, beaming and shuffling all the cards together. 'That's what we're going to be after all.'

We're just getting to the end of a game of Threes, with Aiza sulking because she's not winning by enough cards, when Jessi sways up the carriage towards us. Her eyeshadow glimmers like a peacock's tail and although I'm sure the red strapless top wasn't originally modelled by a forty-one-year-old, it looks good. Her hair pours fleecy down the back of her neck like Momma's used to.

'You look so fancy,' says Ruby.

She nods, looking at us all in a satisfied way. 'I feel about ready for a real night out, for the first time in a while.'

We get to Paddington just before five o'clock, but we've still got a lot of London to get across. The gig is up near Camden, 'in some dive called The Lonesome Dove,' says Jessi. 'Cheesy as hell. Who do they think they are, calling a London pub The Lonesome Dove?'

'A pub?' asks Ruby. 'Will they let us in?'

'They'll let you in,' says Jessi. You can almost see her patting an invisible gun holster.

We all get hungry on the tube. I sort of expect Jessi not to have thought about this and to deal with it by buying a couple of bags of cheese and onion crisps from WH Smith, but she doesn't, she leads us up the warm grey street looking all around her.

'What are you looking for?' I ask, rubbing my belly, which has started growling even though it's only just past six.

'I'm not looking. I'm sniffing. I'm following my nose.'

Jessi's nose leads us to a tiny underground Brazilian restaurant, where three waiters who might be each other's father, grandfather and son dance around Jessi, looking down her top, and we have to wait forty-five minutes for our food, but when it comes it's worth it, although Ruby's chicken strips are so spicy that her eyes fill with tears.

'You don't have to eat them,' says Jessi.

'I love them,' says Ruby, sticking her tongue into her glass of Coke and then shovelling in more chicken.

'No way,' says the man on the door.

'Ah, come on.'

'It's more than my licence is worth.'

'I'll tell you what your licence is worth,' says Jessi.

'Look, love, there's no way anybody's going to believe that they're not minors.' He points at us. Obviously he's not impressed by our sparkly hair or our lip gloss. I feel like I'm letting the side down, though it's not my fault that none of us is six inches taller with boobs.

'Listen,' says Jessi, leaning her elbows on his table, 'I'm a friend of Joe Dillon's.'

'Oh yes?'

'From way back. Grew up in the next neighbourhood over. Now I haven't seen him in years, and I want to introduce him to my daughter, and her friends are along too, and can't you and I work this thing out?'

They look at each other.

'I haven't got time to keep an eye on them all night,' he says.

'You won't need to. I give you a cast-iron guarantee they won't misbehave in any way at all.'

'They won't be drinking.'

'Of course they won't be drinking. What the hell do I look like to you?'

'Not even Coke,' he says flatly. 'I don't want them anywhere near the bar.'

'Sure.'

'In fact they'd have to sit at the other side. Sit. I'm not having them get trampled, or lost, or anything.'

'That ain't my plan neither.'

'If I see them, hear them, or hear anything about them, they're out,' he says.

'Fair enough. And can I skiddle back and introduce them to Joe?'

'You can do what you want after hours,' he says. 'Though I wouldn't if it was my kids.'

All in all it doesn't sound like it's going to be that much fun, but we all cheer in low voices as we walk into the bar.

'I don't know how you got him to let us in,' says Aiza.

'I knew it would be fine.' Jessi stops and drops her bag on the floor while she takes a look around.

'How?' demands Aiza.

'Oh, it's easy. With some men you cry, with some you plead a little, with some you boss them while you flutter your eyelashes.'

I'm not sure this is the kind of lesson that Momma wanted me to get taught, and I can see Gemma's face if she was here.

'In any case,' Jessi finishes, over her shoulder as she heads towards the bar, 'wear red and show a little flesh and you can't go too far wrong.'

For what feels like a long time we sit in a tight little triangle of chairs, trying not to catch anyone's eye or look conspicuous. The place fills up and Aiza, who has her back to the room, goes full deer-in-the-wild startled every time someone takes a step in our direction. I get a bit sleepy. It's not like it's late, only about half eight, it's just that because we might as well be underground – there aren't any windows – it could be any time. Also, the middle of my body is all weighed down with steak and rice and peppers and chocolate and my head feels heavy too. Ruby stretches her eyes so wide every few minutes that I think I'm not the only one feeling dozy.

Jessi comes over with a tray just as a white-faced girl drifts on to the stage, followed by a hairy man.

'Here you are,' she shouts over the whine of the microphone, handing us each a Coke with melty pieces of ice bobbing. 'You excited?'

We all nod with various degrees of speed. 'What are you having?' Aiza yells back, eyeing Jessi's drink, which looks out of place.

'Pineapple juice,' she shouts, hooking another stool with her foot and dragging it over.

'Really?'

'With just a little dash of tequila to pep it up. Oh, come on,' she howls at the stage.

The girl and the bloke finally decide their guitars are in tune, and start singing. It's bad. I can't make out the words properly but she seems to be going on about mermaids or something. Or maybe I'm just confused because she has a tattoo of a mermaid on her arm, which I think has her own face on it.

'The problem with everybody having tattoos these days,' Jessi says perfectly clearly in the moment of silence after the racket ends, 'is that everybody now thinks they're a rock star.'

There's a bit of clapping, not much. The girl tells us that they're really really honoured and grateful to be supporting Joe Dillon, and that they're all the way from the Isle of Man. Then the bearded man pipes up and says that that's the British equivalent of Texas.

I have a feeling that joke would have gone down better in the Isle of Man.

'What is the Isle of Man?' asks Ruby.

The second song isn't any better. In the middle of it a man

161

comes up and starts talking to Jessi. She seems to know him. My ears are beginning to hurt.

'Seriously though,' says Ruby as the song ends, 'what is the Isle of Man?'

'It's where Manx cats come from,' I say, watching Jessi. She's laughing and putting her hand on the man's chest. 'You know, the ones with no legs.'

'Oh,' says Ruby.

'The ones with no legs, Dallas?' says Aiza. 'Really?'

'I meant no tails.'

'And you just accepted it, Rubes,' says Aiza. 'An island full of cats with no legs. I don't know why I'm friends with you two.'

'So that you can feel superior, why else?' says Jessi. 'Girls, I want you to meet Mickey. He bought you your drinks, so be polite. Mickey, this is my girl.' She puts her arm round my shoulders. 'This is Dallas.'

I don't much like the look of Mickey. He's a bit thick in the neck. He's also wearing a white shirt, which shows the sweat.

'So,' he shouts, because the pair on stage are starting again, 'you're taking a first look at the world of rock and roll!'

'Sure,' I say, 'whatever.'

'You're a lucky girl.'

I smile, fast, and turn to the stage.

It turns out I don't have to worry about Mickey, because just after he stumbles back from the bar with more drinks,

Jessi spots somebody she actually knows through the crowd and darts off, and Mickey only stays near us for the length of another song, shouting the odd sentence apologetically, before he gets the message and rambles off.

'Your aunt's cold,' Aiza says, transferring the ice cubes out of her new drink into her old glass.

The two on stage finish and go away to tepid applause. There's loads of people here now – mostly men and mostly quite old and large – and you can't even see the bar. There seems to be a thin ring of power around us, because nobody is coming too close. Then Jessi reappears from out of the crowd with another man. This one is better, I suppose. He's thin and Gemma would say he's broody-looking. Besides, he's wearing a leather jacket that actually fits him.

Jessi introduces him as Pete. She's quite radiant. It turns out he's the bassist for Joe Dillon and she's met him a couple of times. They saunter off together in the direction of the bar.

'If I drink any more Coke I'm going to be weeing all the way home,' says Ruby.

Jessi reappears after a while, with another 'pineapple juice' but thankfully no more Coke. She says Pete had to go and get ready and they'll be on in a second. I'm thankful to hear it. It's getting on for ten o'clock and I'm sleepy, not to mention being sixty miles away from home.

Then everything rumbles, a whole band walks on to the stage and starts playing so loud my collarbones thud, and with a roar from the crowd Joe Dillon appears at the front, grabs the microphone, throws it up in the air and catches it, and sings.

I've been to gigs before, mostly out of doors, Momma used to take us, never anybody famous but you wouldn't expect being famous to make such a difference – especially the kind I assumed Joe Dillon was, the kind I hadn't heard of. This is different. It's big, loud, bluesy rock. I can't stay sitting down to it, and neither can the other two. We get up off our stools. After a couple of songs I look round and the stools have disappeared. Ruby takes hold of the back of my T-shirt, and I don't mind. She's got Aiza's in her other hand.

Joe Dillon is a big man. He's not slim. He's hairy and he's wearing a waistcoat, not to mention the fact that he's super-old. But he's cool and somehow I don't mind looking at him at all while I'm listening to him singing.

We don't know the songs of course. Jessi seems to know them, at least she's singing most of the time, roaring with her eyes closed. Then he plays 'No Place to Fall' by Townes Van Zandt and it's, like, transcendent. I sing but only under my breath because I want to hear. When it gets to the end Ruby touches me on the arm, and I look round and realise that there are tears pouring down my face.

Jessi reaches out and pulls me against her.

I don't want it to end, even though I need a wee, and even though the crowd is thicker and thicker and I'm glad Ruby has a hold of me and I can rely on her to have a hold of Aiza too. She's leaping up and down behind me. I'm slightly stuck to the leather jacket of the man in front of me, but even that's OK. When it stops I could cry again, in fact I do cry again, but Jessi smiles, and once we've all hollered ourselves hoarse they come back on and do three more. One of them is 'Are You Sure Hank Done It This Way' by Waylon Jennings. It's as if Momma was here.

Then it's really over. The lights go on and the crowd kind of heaves and begins to roll away. We all look at each other, sighing. Beaming.

'Let's go get some merch!' Jessi yells, plunging off.

We all follow her. I've got a little bit of money. Aiza has loads and lends Ruby some. I buy the CD Jessi most recommends; Aiza buys two other ones. We agree, quietly, to swap them so we can burn each other's. Ruby wants a T-shirt.

'I don't have 'em in your size, honey,' says the drummer, who's selling them.

'I don't care,' she says.

Then Aiza and I have to admit we want them too so we all buy a T-shirt. Black, with a train on it. Mine comes down to my knees.

'We can wear them to bed,' says Aiza, tucking hers into her bag.

Then there's another roar as Joe Dillon and the rest of his band come out. We queue up to get our stuff signed, me and Aiza digging each other in the ribs to be first and then, as we get close to the front of the queue, getting shy and digging each other to be second. Ruby stands serenely behind us. I lose and end up being first. Joe Dillon looks at me from under crooked eyebrows as he takes my CD.

'You're a little bit younger than most of my core audience,' he says.

'Yes,' I say, 'I suppose so.'

'I'm surprised they let you in.'

'I can be persuasive,' I say.

He laughs. 'What's your name?'

'Dallas.'

'For real? What are you doing in a place like this, Dallas?' He passes me the CD back.

'Learning,' I say.

'And did you and your henchgirls enjoy it?' he asks, taking the CDs Aiza passes him.

'Yes,' Aiza and I say together.

'It was the best thing that's ever happened to me,' says Ruby.

'Dallas,' Jessi says, running up as we stand waiting by the exit sign, clutching everything we've bought, 'we've been invited to stay for the after-party.'

'What?' I say.

She tells us that Joe Dillon remembers her from when they met before, and Pete wants her to stay, and it's a great opportunity and will be a lot of fun, and she knows we're tired but if we can give her another hour or even half an hour then it'll be something we remember and can tell our kids about.

Actually we don't specially need that much convincing. We all know we're about to be really tired and to wish that home was closer, but we're buzzing still.

'You're incredible, girls,' says Jessi. 'Now stand over here. They know I've got you, but nobody wants to feel guilty about kids being present.'

We don't see much for anybody to feel guilty about. We're just standing in the bar, while the man who resentfully let us in all those hours ago moves tables about and sets chairs out and casts sour glances at us. The drummer sits by the bar drinking beer and talking to two women. Everybody else, including Jessi, seems to have vanished through the door by the stage.

'Shall we help?' Ruby says after a while.

We follow the man to the doorway where the tables are stacked, and take one off the top. He grunts. 'Over by the bar,' he says, 'and don't drop it on your foot.'

We carry tables and chairs about. It's OK. The drummer smiles at us and says we're obviously roadies in the making, and when the place looks like a pub again, the bouncer man grunts and gives us a Flake each.

'What time is it?' Ruby asks as she finishes hers.

It's half past twelve. I'm not used to being up this late. Gemma is a bit square about bedtimes and to be honest, Momma used to be too. My face feels the most tired.

'Look,' says the bouncer man, 'this is no place for you lot at this time of night. What's your mother doing?'

I don't say she's not my mother because how complicated. 'I suppose she's mingling.'

'Can't you call her?' Aiza murmurs.

'No, I left my phone at school.'

The drummer starts laughing. 'I'll go and see, all right?'

'You know, we've missed the last train,' Aiza says.

Silence.

'We can get the bus,' I point out. There's a coach up from London to Oxford that runs all night, every half an hour or so. It's how Sam gets back from London when he and Prue go out there.

Aiza checks the time on her phone.

'Oh look,' she says, 'loads of missed calls.' She taps the phone. 'From Dad.' She dials her answerphone.

'What a good night,' Ruby says.

'I hope we get to stay off school tomorrow,' I say.

'Do you think we will?'

'Well, we're meant to be there in eight hours, and we have to get home and stuff, so it's not like we'll be well rested.'

'Yeah,' Ruby says, yawning. 'I hope there's some bread left at home. You know what I had for breakfast this morning? Only I didn't because it was disgusting.'

'What?'

'My mum brought two of them back from the pub – she

said it was all that got left over. She tried to make me eat it but I said she had to eat hers first, and she gagged on it.'

'What?'

'Black-pudding Scotch eggs.'

'Ew,' I say.

'*And* they were duck eggs.'

'Gross.'

Ruby nods. 'That's what fancy people eat. My mum says they scoff them like they're popcorn.'

'Dallas,' Aiza says. 'My dad's left me about a trillion messages.'

'How come?'

'Seems like he's not sure where I am.'

'What? Jessi said she sorted it out with him.'

'Yeah, but – she told him it was a concert and he thought it was just in Oxford and then we'd be staying at yours, only Gemma rang him up and told him she's got no idea where any of us have gone.'

'Oh Christ,' I say. 'Are you going to ring him?'

'I think I'd better wait till Jessi gets back and I can tell him we're on our way home.'

'I can't find her,' says the drummer.

'What?'

He looks alarmed. 'Look, calm down, I'm pretty sure she'll just have gone out for a smoke, is all.'

That sounds likely. That sounds like the most likely explanation. The trouble is that the bouncer man has heard and the bouncer man is not keen on having unattended children in his bar area at one o'clock at night.

'Well, you can't kick them out,' the drummer says.

'Isn't there anyone back there who can come and look after them?'

'Erm. No,' says the drummer.

'Can I go back and look?' I ask. 'I mean, are you sure you're looking for the right person?'

He is sure. He says there's no way he could have missed her. He says he even stuck his head out the back door and he couldn't see her.

'Where's she gone?' the bouncer growls. I don't think he's angry with us exactly, but he's not pleased.

'For a smoke,' the drummer says. They stare at each other over our heads. 'She'll most likely be back any minute.'

'And what if she isn't? I can't have these kids here after hours, this could lose me my licence. She could have gone anywhere.'

The drummer shrugs.

The bouncer squats down. This is how adults try to relate to children. Of course it makes him about two foot shorter than us, but whatever. 'Where do you girls live?'

'Not far,' says Ruby.

'And is there anyone at home right now?'

'Yes,' says Ruby, which is true.

'If we call you a cab then and send you home, you'll be all right?'

'Yes,' says Ruby.

I stay silent because I'm expecting Jessi to turn up. Aiza's distracted by her dad's messages, which she keeps deleting one by one with a grim expression. After a while the phone goes, and as the bouncer has gone off somewhere the drummer answers it, and says that the cab's outside, and comes out with us. We all climb into the back seat.

'Where to?' the driver says in a bored voice.

'Victoria,' says Ruby.

'Thank you,' we say to the drummer, and he shuts the door and pats it and waves.

'What a nice man,' says Ruby.

'Ruby,' I say, 'are we getting the bus home on our own?'

'Yes.'

'What'll we do when we get to Oxford?'

'Oh, we can walk if we have to.'

'Gemma will flip. She'll murder Jessi.' Silence tells me that Ruby and Aiza don't care about that as much as I do. 'And what about money for tickets?'

'I can get some money out,' says Aiza. 'I've still got forty pounds in my account.'

I have a terrible thought. 'What about paying the taxi fare?' I whisper.

We look at each other.

'Isn't it paid?' says Aiza.

'Who would have paid it?'

'I don't know – that man, maybe, to get us out of the bar.'

'Maybe,' I say doubtfully. 'But he wasn't there when it arrived.'

'Maybe he has an account or something.'

Ruby leans forward. 'Excuse me,' she chirrups. 'Has this taxi been paid for?'

The cab screeches to a halt.

It turns out the taxi driver isn't a fan of unpaid fares, and unlike the bouncer he isn't careful about asking us whether we'll be OK. He isn't one to worry about unaccompanied eleven-year-old girls on dark streets either. He dumps us right out and drives off, fast.

'Well!' says Ruby. 'What are we going to do now?'

We can't go back to the bar, we decide.

We don't ring home. This is an unselfish gesture by us. We decide that if Gemma, or Aiza's dad, knew we were standing on an unknown street corner in the middle of London at one thirty in the morning, they might actually literally die of a heart attack.

We decide we'd better walk to Victoria.

It's not that hard. Aiza has her super-smart smartphone that shows us a beautiful map of London, with a route mapped out from Aiza's feet right to Victoria, which it predicts will take us barely more than an hour to walk. It's a warm night. We're all wearing trainers. We're going to be fine.

'So,' Aiza says, 'black-pudding duck eggs.'

'Yep.'

'What else do they eat?'

'Ox cheeks,' says Ruby. 'And pigeon on toast.'

'That's disgusting.'

You would think it would be spooky, but it isn't. For one thing it's so much brighter than Oxford is at night, and it's all big roads after all, it's not like we're creeping down alleyways. A long way past Regent's Park, which keeps Ruby happy talking about *101 Dalmations*. A long way up Regent Street, looking at the shops. We're all getting a bit floppy now. All that meat and chocolate is still in a ball in my stomach and yet I think I'm hungry. Everybody's quiet. I'm worried that they're blaming me for this, because of Jessi, because it's hard not to blame her. If only I hadn't forgotten my stupid phone so I could ring her, or if I knew her number so I could ring her from Ruby's . . . I know Gemma's number, I know Sam's, why don't I know Jessi's? And Momma always used to make sure all my friends had her number stored, when she took us places. Why didn't I remember that till now? Still, as long as we can go on putting one foot in front of another, and as long as we keep avoiding people's eyes and nobody notices us enough to interfere, then sometime we're going to get to Victoria. And sometime there'll be a bus home.

Up Conduit Street and across Piccadilly – it's amazing how many people there are around at almost three o'clock in the morning – and past Green Park – if it was up to me I'd probably be stupid or tired enough to go through it but

Ruby says no – and around to the Mall. Past a big memorial to Queen Victoria and 'Is that Buckingham Palace?' Ruby asks.

We all look up.

'It looks like a big barn,' says Ruby.

Down a long street, and putting one foot in front of another is getting harder now, but the sky is also almost light, and there are people now in suits who look like they might be on their way to work, though who starts work at not long past three a.m., as well as the wrecked-looking ones drifting out of nightclubs.

'McDonald's,' says Ruby, but I don't look.

And there's Victoria. I know where the Oxford Tube stops, this is where we come when we're shopping in London or going to a museum or a theatre. I take them, feet throbbing, just past the station and over the road and there's the bus stop. And as we limp up to it, there's a rushing sound and an Oxford Tube bus sweeps past us and stops.

The driver won't let us on.

'Please,' I say.

'No chance, love,' he says.

'But we're eleven,' I say, stupidly.

'And what you're doing out on your own at this time, I don't know.'

'We live in Oxford,' Ruby explains.

'And how am I supposed to know if that's true, you could be running away for all I know. I should call the police.'

'Dallas,' Ruby says, 'you're going to have to ring home.'

'Oh God.'

'It's true, Dallas,' Aiza says.

I know Gemma's number. I also know Sam's. I consider who is best to ring at half past three on a night when they may or may not genuinely think that I'm a missing person.

'Hello?'

'Sam,' I say, 'it's me.'

I listen to him shouting. Then Gemma seizes the phone and shouts some more, less in anger than as if she thinks I might not actually be able to hear her, or I might be in the process of falling off a cliff. 'Stay there. Do you hear me? Till I call you back. Right at the bus stop. I'm going to ring Jessi and she'll get to you as fast as she possibly can.'

Which she does. She falls out of a cab about fifteen minutes later, just as we're all getting really cold, and comes racing up to us. She's distraught. She's also furious.

'What the hell were you doing, leaving that bar on your own?'

'The man told us to,' I say feebly.

She shouts a bit more.

I don't have anything to add, but Aiza does. She starts shouting too, just as another Oxford Tube draws up. 'We didn't know where you were, OK. I mean, you just left us there and then you disappeared. And my dad was leaving me frantic messages because he didn't know where we were either, because you told him we'd be in Oxford and then apparently didn't tell Gemma anything at all.'

Jessi pipes down. She pushes us all to the back seat downstairs and sits two rows in front with her arms crossed, although when some more people get on at Shepherd's Bush she moves back one.

Aiza sits down in the middle and fumes. Ruby leans against the window and shuts her eyes straight away. Aiza pokes her.

'Aren't you worried about your mum?'

'No,' Ruby says, without opening her eyes.

About a second later she starts snoring. Aiza stares straight ahead. I lean on the other window and don't say anything, because everybody's in such a bad mood and I'm annoyed with Aiza for yelling at Jessi after she gave us this big treat, and I'm obviously annoyed at Jessi, and I'm embarrassed because we did the wrong thing, and I'm exhausted, and I'm freaked out by what's coming. Because I don't think Gemma is going to be pleased.

Half-waking when the bus pulls into Lewknor Turn and the driver shouts 'Lewwwwwknor' is so miserable that I go back to sleep, which makes waking up properly when he gets to the Park and Ride even worse. I feel like all the juice has been squished out of me, except maybe for a hard ball of meat in my stomach. And I'm cold, and I need a wee quite badly, which makes sense because when I think about it it's been about eight hours since I last went. Although that's standard for a night, and maybe it isn't all that different just because you happen to be up and about instead of asleep in bed . . .

'Dallas,' says Ruby, and points out of the window as the bus draws up at St Aldate's. Gemma is there, and Aiza's dad.

I don't know what I'm expecting any more, but Gemma more or less envelops me. I don't remember ever being hugged so tight in my life, even though it's only for a second, because then she grabs Ruby as Ruby steps down. The bus shuts its doors crossly behind us.

13

Aiza's dad takes Ruby, and I'm glad, because Aiza has a whole bed for her, and also I can tell that this isn't going to be the kind of row that gets politely put off because we have a guest. It's barely put off long enough for us all to get into Aiza's dad's illegally parked car and for him to drive us to the road end of the track down to the towpath.

I'm sure Gemma wakes up a few of the barge families, but it's nothing to when we get inside the boathouse and Sam's waiting.

While Sam and Jessi shout at each other, Gemma cooks sausages and toast and serves me first and then Billy and Violet, who are all excitable about being up so early. I don't want sausages, I'm virtually asleep at the table even with all the yelling.

'Why did you run away?' Violet whispers to me.

'I didn't,' I whisper back. 'I just went to a concert.'

'Can I come to a concert too?' Billy asks, stealing a sausage from my plate and offering me a toast crust in return.

On the whole I'm surprised how well Jessi is taking it. She sits through about a million uses of the words 'irresponsible' and 'reckless', and Sam telling her over and over about how me and my friends could have been kidnapped and trafficked and ended up on Gumtree, whatever that means. I'm hoping that I might get to go to bed before I get killed.

It's when Gemma interrupts Sam – 'OK, we may as well stop now. Jessi's just not used to being responsible for children, or thinking that way' – that Jessi snaps.

'She's never even here,' she's yelling five minutes later. 'Have you noticed that? Doesn't that tell you something, or don't you have time to worry about Dallas?'

'Of course I worry about Dallas,' says Gemma in a stilted voice.

'The child is wandering the city instead of coming home. Crying every time she's on her own . . .'

'Don't try and turn this around,' Sam says, but neither of them even look at him.

'Of course she cries every time she's on her own,' Gemma says. 'Don't you? And the being out – it's her way of grieving. She hasn't dealt with Rosa not being here yet, she has to come to terms with that in her own time. She's happy at Aiza's, she's comfortable there . . .'

'You don't think there's something wrong when an eleven-year-old kid is comfortable at some other kid's house and not at home? How can she be happy here, when none of you have time for her. You're always with Violet, Sam's all caught up in Billy, nobody ever gives a thought to Dallas.'

'Look,' Gemma shouts, 'I spend every waking moment

worrying about one member of this family or another. I've taken advice, we've all seen counsellors, they've told me to let her go for a while as long as she has a safe place to be – I said, isn't it a risk, that I might lose her, but the counsellor said . . .'

'. . . you can't lose what you never had?' Jessi says.

We all wince.

'Look,' she says, 'I don't want it to get nasty. We're all worried about . . . everyone. Right now we're talking about Dallas. She needs a lot of support and none of you are in a position to give that to her.'

'I suppose you are,' Sam snarls.

'Which is why,' Jessi says, ignoring them, and my stomach knots up so fast I nearly lose the sausages, 'I'm taking her back to Texas with me when I go.'

Pause.

'To Texas?' says Gemma.

'To Austin, yeah.'

Pause.

'Is Dallas going to America?' Violet asks Gemma, sounding disbelieving. 'To live?' I suppose she thinks I'll be next-door neighbours with Minnie Mouse or something.

'No, she isn't,' says Sam.

'You can't do that, Jessi,' says Gemma. 'You can't make promises like that to Dallas, that's not fair on her. Look, you should have come to me first.'

Violet starts to cry.

'I feel like it concerns Dallas . . .'

'You're not taking her to Texas,' says Sam. 'Not even for a week. Not for a weekend even.'

Gemma and Jessi ignore Sam, like they're ignoring me. 'I'm her legal guardian,' says Gemma.

'For now you are.'

'What's that supposed to mean?'

'Dallas still has a father,' says Jessi, 'like she still has an aunt, and a grandmother.'

'I'm her legal guardian.'

'Because her father said you could be. But I spoke to him last week.' They don't take their eyes off each other. Billy's crying now as well. 'He said he thought this should be up to Dallas. If they ask him, that's what he'll say.'

Sam gets up so fast that his plate goes flying across the table and crashes on to the floor. Violet shrieks. Billy runs into the corner. 'I'm going to kill him,' Sam says.

'Sit down,' says Gemma.

'Not content with everything he's done,' Sam says, 'and now he sells Dallas.'

Gemma kicks Sam and Jessi out of the house. Tells them not to come back till they've cooled off and I've had a chance to sleep.

'Are you really going away, Dallas?' Violet whispers as we listen to them all shouting just outside.

I pass her the tissue box. 'I don't know.'

181

'Why?'

'It might make things easier,' I say. Then I feel bad, and I squat down next to her. 'Listen, if I do, you'll still see me. Holidays, and things. You can come and see me in Texas and ride a horse if you want.'

She's got big green eyes that I forget about until I'm close up. She uses them to look at me like I'm a swindler, and goes around Gemma's screen to lie down on the bed where I can't see her.

'What's wrong?' Billy says, climbing on my knee.

'It's all right,' I tell him. 'Nothing.'

He tucks his head under my chin. I can feel his heart beating.

Gemma comes back in and makes me go to bed. Even though my brain is reeling like a broken bike wheel, the moment I lie down I fall asleep. I think I'm safe from having to go to school anyway.

Hours and hours later, I'm woken by a WhatsApp from Ruby.

Have you seen the paper

I get up and go downstairs. Nobody's there. I ride my bike down to the newsagent's, feeling like I washed my face in thick soap and didn't rinse it afterwards, and flick through the local paper. There's a picture of me in it, with half of Ruby's face and the back of Aiza's head, holding up my placard. I look worried, podgy and about eight.

TRAGIC SCHOOLGIRL LIBRARY CAMPAIGN,
the headline reads.

I shut the paper, take it to the counter, pay for it and cycle home, where I leave it on the table, put the kettle on and go for a wee. Only when I'm sitting at the table with a cup of tea do I open it up again.

Dallas Kelly knows more about loss than most girls her age, the article reads. *Her beloved mum was killed in a road accident last October, leaving three children. Dallas (just 11 years old) admits that she misses her activist mum every day. But she has found a cause she knows her mum would feel passionately about – the local library.*

'My mother loved books and so do I,' Dallas tells me. 'Libraries are important for everyone but specially for kids.'

It's hard to argue with that, yet the council have slashed library funding to the bone in the last few years. Queen Street library, Dallas's local branch, is due to shut down at the end of next week, and your reporter has learned that Saxon Homes has put in a seven-figure offer for the site on which they plan to build a block of tasteful luxury apartments. 'It's so unfair,' says Dallas. 'Why should we have to lose out?'

When asked to comment, the leader of the council, Ophelia Silk, said that in the current climate cuts have to be made. 'It's a question of priority,' she says. 'I feel for the residents who will be affected, but not many people use the Queen Street branch and we have to make decisions based on need across the city.' No comments were offered by Silk on the sale of the site, and she brushed aside a question about how she would explain her position to an 11-year-old. 'When you actually engage people in debate on this issue, you find that they haven't understood the facts.'

We would love to see the stern Mrs Silk engage dewy-eyed Dallas Kelly in debate. Everybody might learn something.

Well, that's humiliating, I think, rereading the things I'm supposed to have said. I sound like I'm talking in a foreign language. I never said 'why should we have to lose out'.

Oh God I WhatsApp Ruby and Aiza. *I sound like a git*
Yeah you do Aiza messages back. *This is not cool*
Photo tho! Ruby taps.

There's a pause. I'm rereading the whole thing. Wondering if it's online and, if so, if there'll be comments underneath. I get another message from Aiza in the middle of it.

Guys this will not stand. Going to have to do something about this now.

Sam says the piece is fine and what was I expecting. He's not concentrating though. I think Gemma must have told him to lay off me because he's walking round tapping everything with his fingers and avoiding me, which is fine because I can't look him in the eye either. It's hateful hurting people. Gemma says I should be proud of the interview. Jessi cuts the picture out and puts it in her wallet. Gemma sends Sam out to buy another copy.

I catch Gemma doctoring the paper with a Sharpie.

When she reads it out to Billy and Violet she misses the part about Momma leaving three children.

'I'm not having it,' Aiza says. Like me, she and Ruby are still a bit puffy and bug-eyed looking. 'They're not getting away with this crap.'

I don't exactly follow.

'Calling you eleven all the time.'

'She is eleven,' Ruby says.

'Yeah, but like we're just kids. And that woman at the council, saying you're thick. I'm not having it. We've got to sort it out now.'

'Sort what out?' My brain is fogged.

'The library. Let's get your act together and fix the library thing.'

Aiza goes to Mr Chaplin and then to Ms O'Leary, via Ms Wilson, and gets them all to basically say that we can do what we like to save the library. She drags us round every single class and the staff room to tell people all about the library. She sets up an online petition, and then we go around again and tell them all to sign it. I think about mentioning that Momma hated online petitions and used to get in rows about it all the time with people, but I decide against it. It's best not to get in front of Aiza when she's in a horn-tossing mood.

She makes me write a piece about the campaign for the school newsletter, then she makes Ms Wilson and Mr

Chaplin read it and tell me how to make it better. She makes Ms Wilson stop doing the letter she's supposed to be sending to Year 3 parents about remembering to pay for their trip to the arboretum, and put my piece on the website instead. Then she makes Ms Wilson email all the parents, in the whole school, with a link to it.

Then she goes to Mr West and asks him to send it to any famous journalists he knows. Mr West does the creative writing club and has a beard. Mr West says that funnily enough he doesn't have many journalists of national stature for close friends but he'll give it some thought.

Finally Aiza drags us back into the office to see if Ms Wilson's had any good replies from parents to the email, and we find Libby, Jada and Sophie there talking to Ms O'Leary about how they'd like to donate the proceeds from tomorrow's cake sale to the library campaign.

'What for?' says Aiza.

'To help keep it open, of course,' says Libby. 'It's our library too, Aiza.'

'No it isn't,' says Ruby. 'You all live closer to Jericho.'

'I don't,' says Sophie.

'You didn't care about it last week when Dallas did her assembly,' Aiza says.

'That's what we call a slow burn, Aiza,' says Ms O'Leary. 'Now if you girls all work together, I wouldn't dare to put a limit on what you can accomplish.'

As we leave the office, Aiza snorts.

'Ahhh,' says Libby. 'Did you want to keep the library all to yourself?'

'Obviously not,' I say. 'It's a public library.'

'What was the cake sale going to be for?' asks Ruby.

'Disadvantaged children. We explained to Ms O'Leary how the library thing is totally for disadvantaged children too though,' Libby says. 'You know, Ruby. Disadvantaged children like you?'

'What?' says Ruby.

'Ignore her, Rubes,' says Aiza, lunging at Libby's hair, which is hanging over her shoulder like a fat brown snake, but she's too quick and is in the classroom already.

After lunch when we go into the office to check on things, Ms Wilson tells us she's had three messages of support from parents since she sent that email. She also asks us if we've seen the paper's website since this morning, and gets it up on screen for us.

There are a ton of comments on the piece. One person calls it exploitation – 'of you, that means,' Aiza says – and another talks about PC culture and having to make tough decisions, but there are some good ones too, from people who use Queen Street library, and even one which says how heartening it is to see children getting stuck in like we are. And there's one which says how good it would be if there was a debate, like the reporter suggested. With Ophelia Silk. And me.

I nudge Aiza, who's stuck on the comment that says how pathetic it is for newspapers to pretend a story is about anything other than middle-class preoccupations, just by sticking half a non-white child in the picture – I suppose this must mean Aiza. People are so weird. Imagine writing a comment like that. 'Look,' I say.

'What?'

'Annaliese from Cowley says I should debate with the council leader. Can you imagine?'

'Don't worry about Annaliese from Cowley,' Aiza says. 'It's David from Witney that's the problem,' and she goes back to her letter.

Ms Wilson switches page to the editorial. Where there's a long paragraph by the editor calling on Ophelia Silk to meet me for a debate on the fate of Queen Street library.

'Nobody's going to make you do a debate with an adult, Dallas,' Aiza says. 'Stop reading that crap and help us get ideas.'

'Ideas about what?' I ask absently, following her out of the office.

'What we're going to do to the cake sale, of course,' says Aiza. 'Ruby says we should use water again. Mr Elgin might have the sprinklers on if it's hot.'

'They don't like water,' says Ruby.

'Indeed they do not. But it would be better not to get into loads of trouble if we can avoid it, so I was thinking . . .'

'Oh, leave it,' I say. 'Leave them alone this time.'

'Dallas Kelly, do my ears deceive me?'

I think about what Sam said, about bullies. 'Look,' I say, 'I know Libby's horrible. But she just wants to be in charge, that's why she's horned in on this. And in the end it's for the library, isn't it. If we ruin it then there won't be any money raised.'

'We're talking about maybe fifty quid. What are you going to do, keep the library open for half an hour longer?'

'Don't worry about it,' Sam says. 'She won't want to debate with you. Look at it from her point of view. If she destroys you, which she would, then she'll look like a cold-hearted monster. And if you manage to say even one sensible or adorable thing, the paper will run with it. Wash Billy's hands in the kitchen for me, will you, I need a slash.' He doesn't look me in the face. He hasn't looked me in the face in days.

'Dallas,' says Gemma, dishing out lasagne, 'I've got something to tell you.'

I look up from the garlic bread plate, which I'm hanging on to to stop Billy emptying it on to his own.

'I got a call today from Ophelia Silk.'

'Oh God.'

'It's not bad. She wants to meet you again. Have a chat.'

'Oh *God.*'

'No, no. It's not a debate. She doesn't want a debate. A debate would be ridiculous, we all know that. But if she can say she's had a proper chat with you, where you both talk about things, then she'll look better in the paper.'

'Silly season,' says Sam, sitting down. 'Dallas, put the garlic bread down.'

'Stop looking so haunted, Dallas,' says Gemma. 'Surely you can manage a conversation, can't you? Talking of which. It's time we all had a talk.'

'More than time,' says Sam, glowering.

'The last thing we want, Dallas, is for you to think we're ganging up on you . . .'

I lose my appetite.

'What I want to know,' Sam says, 'is what you think you're doing.'

'Sam,' Gemma says, 'gently, please. We agreed.'

'I just don't get what the attraction is. That ditzy, irresponsible cow as your only family? Is that really what you want?'

'Don't call her that.'

'No, don't,' says Gemma.

Billy casts about six chunks of garlic bread high into the air.

'Ugh,' says Violet. 'I hate lasagne.'

'Hey, you all,' says Jessi, coming in. 'I just dropped by to ask if Dallas could come spend the night with me tomorrow.'

'I don't know,' Gemma says, picking crumbs of garlic out of her hair.

Sam lobs two bread chunks back on to the table. 'What if you lose her again?'

Jessi smiles. 'I won't even let her take a pee on her own, OK?'

'As long as you don't run off to Texas,' Sam says, leaving the table.

I go up to get my nightie before I have a shower, and he's sitting on his bed, staring out of the window. He's not even playing his guitar. Billy is watching him anxiously.

'All right?' I say, pausing in the doorway.

'Why are you doing what she says?' he asks me. 'Because I know you don't really want to go and live with her.'

I stand on one foot. 'She needs me,' I say in the end.

'You're an idiot,' he says, and gently pushes Billy out so he can slam the door in my face.

Billy headbutts me in the stomach and puts his arms round my waist. I sit down with him for a minute, wishing Sam had said, 'We need you too . . .'

'I can't believe they're going to make you do that,' says Ruby on Friday.

I shrug. 'Gemma says, if I don't it looks like I'm not that bothered, and it gives the high ground back to her. Ophelia Silk.'

'But what are you going to talk about?'

'I don't know. I don't think it matters much. It's not like

I'm going to convince her to keep it open by the force of my arguments.'

'Maybe you'll just talk about *Hollyoaks* then,' says Aiza. 'When is it?'

'Tomorrow morning,' I say glumly. 'At the library.'

'Never mind, how bad can it be? Do you want to come over tonight? Ruby's coming. Dad's out again with *Sofia*. He said we could get pizza. He thinks he can buy me off with cheese, I swear. Well, I'll take the pizza but if he thinks . . .'

'I can't come,' I say. 'I'm camping with Jessi.'

I stick around after school, even though Aiza's a bit huffy with me, to see if Libby and her gang need any help with the cake sale. But the cake sale is halted after two minutes when one of the mothers mentions that the chocolate cupcakes taste odd, and Libby realises that salt has been poured over more or less every cake on the table.

'I just don't know why you'd do that,' I say to Aiza and Ruby, once we've been allowed out of Ms O'Leary's office and are far enough out of school. We all swore blind we knew nothing about it, of course.

'Oh shut up, Dallas,' says Aiza. 'It's no big deal. There's a cake sale every week and they raise sod all, you know that.'

'It's not the point,' I shout. 'You said you were on my side, you said you wanted to save the library, and then you sabotage somebody that's trying to raise money for it. You can be such a git, Aiza. Everything has to be about you.'

'It was about Ruby,' she yells back. 'I don't know if you heard how they talk to her.'

'Yes I have, but what was the point today? Everybody knows it was us, all you've done is made us look like bullies.' They don't know I'm moving to Texas, and for some reason this makes me very angry with them. 'And all this crap about your dad's girlfriend. If you did get a stepmother, so what? You know, when your own mother's gone you should be really glad if somebody else wants to take you on, because you might need that one day, did you ever think of that?'

Then I walk off, because I hate shouting.

Jessi plays me all the songs I ask for, and more besides, while I turn the sausages which take about a million years to cook. It is a beautiful night. When it's dark enough to bed down, Jessi talks again about Texas, and what school will be like there, and what kind of a place we'll rent, but for some reason I can't get Billy off my mind, and the way he hung on to me while I was getting my sleeping bag. And Violet. Gracie asked her today was she looking forward to starting school and she started crying.

I love Jessi, and I love Billy and Sam and Gemma and Violet, and I suppose I love Ruby and Aiza too, and I don't know why that has to be so difficult. I'm tired of things being so difficult.

14

'Now, wouldn't it be great if you and I could work things out,' says Ophelia Silk.

We're sitting at a little table in the garden, which has been shut off for us. Every now and again a face appears at the window. When I arrived half an hour ago Gracie was super anxious. She kept telling me not to worry, that what happens here is just a big 'let's pretend' and will make no difference, and that she's in the throes of setting up a 'read-in' which she's discovered is definitely the best next step. And then Mrs Silk arrived and I got bustled out here and presented with two shortbread biscuits and a cup of tea so strong it makes my teeth curl.

'I do love a good cuppa,' says Ophelia Silk.

She's obviously dressed down and all casual for the occasion. For her this means that her earrings are bigger than usual and that she's got on a soft jersey sort of jacket with gold buttons on it, and jeans that look starched. Good luck to her. I'm wearing hacked-off shorts and an old T-shirt of Sam's with the Tasmanian Devil on it. The tumble dryer at the laundrette wasn't working this morning.

'It's good to meet somebody like you, Dallas,' says Ophelia Silk.

'You mean an eleven-year-old?'

'No. I mean an eleven-year-old who cares so much about something and who's willing to take on adults over it,' she says. 'When you must know that you're going to lose.'

I look up at her, and she's watching me above her cup of tea.

'I bet it's hard,' she says. 'Because I bet your friends don't really understand. Not this, and not what you've been through this last year.'

'They're doing their best,' I say, and crunch my biscuit.

'Good. You know, I don't say this to make you realise we're sisters under the skin, Dallas,' she says, 'but I lost my mother when I was fourteen.' She crunches her shortbread too. It sounds like someone galloping over dead trees. 'And I do remember what it was like. Anyway. What can we do about this mess, do you think?'

'But you don't want to do anything about it,' I say. 'You're here to make it go away.'

She nods. 'True. I don't see how we can possibly keep the place open. I've got about twenty places to put every penny that we get at the council before I get anywhere near the libraries. I don't want to be snide, but nobody has come up with any useful suggestions on how I could actually afford to keep this place open.'

'You need more pennies,' I say.

'Well.'

'That's maths, isn't it.'

'I can't get more pennies right now.'

'Except by selling the library?'

'Touché.' She raises her cup to me. 'But if I can't keep it open, shouldn't I sell it to help keep other libraries open?'

'No. Raise taxes,' I say.

'I can't raise taxes.'

'Of course you can.'

'I can't.'

'Would you if you could?'

'No.' We look at each other across the table. 'I like you, Dallas,' says Ophelia Silk. 'You shoot from the hip.'

'Don't try to distract me with compliments,' I say.

She laughs.

'If people need more stuff,' I say, 'then we need more money to pay for the stuff, so we need to raise taxes. It's obvious.'

'Not to the voter,' says Ophelia Silk, 'and therefore, not to the government. Or the local government.' She leans back in her chair. 'If you want to change that, you're going to have to think bigger.'

'Like being prime minister?' I say.

'Perhaps.'

She tells me some stuff about being a politician, and it's not totally boring, even though I can't stop minding that

I disagree with her on so much stuff. She says if I work hard and look out for luck then maybe I could be prime minister, or anything else I want. Mostly that's what all adults say, but the part about looking out for luck is a bit different. Then she says: 'But in the meantime, Dallas, if you take my advice, you'll start giving up on this. In your head, if not in your actions. I'm not a monster and I don't want to crush an eleven-year-old child.'

'You won't crush me,' I say.

'You and I would both like to save the library, but there's no money. And we do have a basic difference in political philosophy, it seems. Of course right now you're eleven years old and I'm the leader of the council, which makes my political philosophy more relevant than yours.' She looks across at me. 'I'd appreciate it if you didn't tell that reporter I said that.'

'All right,' I say.

'But it's not either of our philosophies that matter right now, it's the political reality. Look, you could go out there and cry salt tears for the papers, and I could wring my hands, and it wouldn't make any difference because there just isn't any money for this library. It's a brutal lesson, Dallas, but it's one everybody in politics has to learn so you may as well hear it now. Sometimes you just have to accept things.'

And then we go out into the main library and a photographer busts a flash in our faces and a different reporter asks me if I'm satisfied and I say, no, and Ophelia

Silk tells them we had a good chat and I get asked if it was a good chat and I say, it was OK. I stand around awkwardly with Gemma on one side of me and Jessi on the other before Billy headbutts me in the belly and Violet comes belting up and says did I save the library, and I look up from them to catch Ophelia Silk's eye just before she leaves, with handshakes on all sides, even with Gracie who then flushes and stamps off because she didn't intend to shake the hand of the oppressor.

'How was it?' asks Sam, dragging Billy away from the open-door button.

'All right,' I say. 'Weird.'

'What did she say?'

'She told me her mother died when she was fourteen.'

Sam snorts. Then he looks sideways and says, 'Look, you've done well. You've done what you could.'

I shrug.

'What you should do now is just enjoy your last week at St John's. You know. You're not going to get it again.'

I nod. And I watch him crouch down so Billy can get on his back. I know he's biting his lip to keep back all the things he wants to say about me going with Jessi. I'll have to listen to it sometime, I know that, and I know it'll be bad, but I'm grateful to him for holding back today.

'Look,' he says, straightening up. He picks a book off the shelf beside him. 'You're probably too young for this – I was thirteen – but I've been saving it for you, and if . . . well. You should read it.'

I look at the book he hands me. *The Outsiders*. 'Why?'

'Just read it, fool,' he says, and hoists Billy a bit higher. 'There's a Dallas in it. An angry Dallas.'

'Oh,' I say thoughtfully.

I sit down, after he's gone. It's a sunny Saturday afternoon, the best time to sit in the library. I open up the book. I've got nothing else to do.

Hours later, Gracie says, 'Dallas,' and it's like sitting up after having your eyes closed and your ears underwater. I blink and stare at her, not sure for a second what time of year it is or who I am. The library is much darker.

'It's closing time,' she tells me. 'Don't worry, I let Gemma know you were here.'

I blink again, and look down at the book I'm still holding open. 'I don't have my library card.'

'Take it,' she says. 'I know where you live.'

I finish the book at just past midnight. I lie in bed and cry and cry, and for the first time I don't feel sick and ashamed while I'm doing it.

There's a big picture of me looking wary and unbelievably scruffy next to Ophelia Silk, beaming in pearls and jeans, on the front of the other local paper on Monday. Sam comes back with it from his pre-breakfast run.

'That's one for the scrapbook,' Gemma says, holding it up to the light.

I eat my breakfast and go to school.

'Not bad,' says Aiza. 'Though you could have looked less like an earthquake victim.'

'I think it's brilliant,' says Ruby.

'Have you stopped sulking yet then?' Aiza asks.

'Get stuffed,' I say, and then they both get me and squash me and Aiza drills me on the collarbone with her knuckles until Mr Chaplin tells us that's a fine example to set to the little ones in our last week and to go inside in a more seemly fashion, please. And the moment we do, Aiza forgives him because he's Blu-tacked the front page of the paper to the whiteboard.

None of the other teachers makes a fuss about it, and Aiza gets in a mood. 'The trouble with the world at the moment,' she says at break, 'is that everybody's addicted to the success story. They don't want to hear about the noble defeat.'

'We haven't been defeated,' I say. 'We're going to be, but it hasn't happened yet.'

'Or even the last ditch stand – not before it happens anyway. What do you mean, it hasn't happened yet? I thought it was definitely closing on Friday?'

'We're going to have a read-in in a couple of days,' I explain. 'Everyone thought we'd better do it while the press might still be interested.'

'Oooh, the *press*,' Libby says, coming round the corner, and Jada snickers. 'What a media star.'

'So,' I say to Aiza and Ruby, 'it'll probably be on Wednesday afternoon, you know, because normally the library shuts at lunchtime on Wednesdays.'

'What happens at it?' Ruby asks.

'Reading,' Libby cuts in, 'so you probably shouldn't bother turning up, Ruby.'

'Not your thing,' says Jada.

'We just read,' I say to Ruby, 'and hopefully someone takes pictures, and we stay as long as we can. I think we're going to order pizza. But Gemma says I have to go home by nine o'clock.'

'And what a loss that'll be,' says Libby.

'Did you want something?' I ask her, because Aiza isn't going to be able to go on ignoring them.

'Yeah,' she says, 'some fashion tips. Although I see you aren't wearing your best T-shirt today.'

There's a pause.

'No,' I say, 'that's true.'

'Why don't you let me give you some fashion tips,' says Aiza.

'Aiza,' Ruby says, 'don't.'

15

By Wednesday the mood at school is weird. Everyone is sort of misty and intense as if it's the last day already. When we practise our songs for the leavers' assembly, people look like they might cry.

'What's wrong?' Aiza asks me.

'Nothing.'

'Oh, Dallas, you're not going to be one of the sappy weepy crowd on Friday are you? Sobbing as you cling on to Mr Chaplin's corduroy trousers?'

'No,' I say.

'Because that would be pathetic.'

'Are you all right?' Ruby asks her, and now that she mentions it Aiza is talking a bit fast. And her eyes are glittering.

'Oh, I'm fine, Rubes. Why wouldn't I be? I'm stuffed full of delicious chicken curry for one thing.'

'You had chicken curry for breakfast?' Ruby asks.

'No no, this was last night's treat. Chicken, I don't know exactly what, but oh so full of butter. Delicately cooked by Sofia, just for me and my dad.'

'What?'

'Oh yes, didn't I tell you yesterday? Oh of course, that would have been because I DIDN'T KNOW YESTERDAY. Yeah. When I got in from school, Dad was there. No Rabia. So I thought, that's nice, daddy/daughter time, only by six I'm starving to death and he says we can't eat because Sofia is coming round for dinner and SHE'S COOKING.'

'What was the food like?' Ruby asks practically.

Aiza howls.

'What was she like?' I ask.

'She's about twenty-five, I swear, all this long hair and long, I don't know, legs or whatever, and big flappy eyelashes. What a gold-digger, it's embarrassing. The curry was fine, Ruby, quite nice, I expect she got her mother to cook it.'

'Were you polite?'

'Of course I was bloody polite. I was polite as all get-out, Dallas. I hung her bag up for her. Had a bit of a dig around in it first, naturally, but she'd hidden everything interesting.'

I decide that if Aiza had to have this trauma, it's a good thing it happened just now, because she won't notice if I'm distracted. Which I am. I've decided to tell Aiza and Ruby about me leaving today, but thinking about actually doing it . . . I'm doubting myself again. Doubting everything. I want hours on a computer to google everything to do with Austin. I want to talk to somebody, really talk.

I don't tell them till cricket. I hate cricket. I'm lurking behind the oak tree trying to look like I'm actually eagerly waiting to catch balls when Ruby suddenly appears beside me. 'What?' I say.

'Oh shut up, Dallas,' says Aiza from my other side. 'It's not like we can't tell when you're sulking.'

Luckily the lesson has degenerated and the cricket coach is busy trying to stop Gilbert Finch and Toby from hitting each other, and Mr Chaplin is sunning himself over near school, so nobody bothers us as we lean up against the wall and I tell them. They don't shout at me. They don't even interrupt. I start waffling about how we'll all be in different classes anyway, even if I stay, till I force myself to shut up.

'Do you want to go?' Aiza asks. Which is kind of refreshing.

'I don't know,' I say.

Ruby stands up on the wall, which is low and topped with big iron railings. She clings to the railings. She has her thinking face on. 'Really?' she asks.

'Really,' I say. 'Like – I feel like there would be good things about it.'

Ruby nods, staring out over the allotments at the back of the school. 'A fresh start and all that.'

'Exactly,' I say, surprised.

Aiza blinks at us both. 'Shut up, Ruby!'

'What?'

'You've got to at least make it hard!'

'Like how?'

'Like this. Er, Dallas? It would definitely be completely

terrible,' says Aiza, 'and you should absolutely certainly stay here.'

I grin.

'I don't want to make it hard,' Ruby says to the sky. 'Not if she wants to go. Things are hard enough, aren't they.'

'She picks now to go all Zen,' Aiza mutters.

Ruby looks down on both of us. 'It's been rubbish lately for Dallas. If this is her break to make things better, she's got to take it. It's obvious. You know that.'

'Hey, Ruby,' hollers Libby from the tarmac. 'We can totally see up your skirt.'

Ruby smooths down her skirt without even flinching, and crouches to get back down.

'They have nasty girls in Texas too,' Aiza tells me.

Ruby stands up again on the wall.

'And it's not a pretty sight,' calls Jada.

Aiza rolls her eyes. We both step up beside Ruby.

'Don't,' she says, in a panicked voice.

'What's wrong?'

'I'm stuck.'

'What?'

'My knee. I can't get it out.'

When she bent her knee to crouch it somehow went between the railings, even though a knee shouldn't do that, because if it can do that then it should come back out again. Which isn't happening.

'Oh God,' she says. 'I can't get down.'

'Chill,' says Aiza, trying to bend the iron railing.

'I'm going to get kicked out. Two days before school finishes.'

The thing is, we're not supposed to climb on this wall. Aiza and I look at each other.

'Don't worry,' I say, and I stick my right foot through. It isn't elegant, I end up kind of straddling the wall with only my left toes touching the playground, but I finally get into a position where I'm sort of stuck. Meanwhile Aiza has literally knotted her hair around one of the railings.

'I will never understand you, girls,' Mr Chaplin says later, as we stand and watch the fireman getting ready to cut off the top of the railings. 'I don't even know if I want to. I think the world might crumble if I once got inside your heads.'

'Never mind, sir,' Aiza says. Her hair is shorter on the left now than on the right, but she says she's due a haircut. 'You'll have a nice boring class next year.'

'I'm looking forward to it,' he agrees.

It's noisy as they cut into the metal. I stop rubbing the outside of my thigh where there's still a railing-shaped dent, and put my hands over my ears. Ruby looks like Joan of Arc waiting for someone to light her woodpile.

'I think we'd better go to my office for a little chat,' says Ms O'Leary, striding over to us.

'Oh, Ms O'Leary,' Aiza says, 'it's the read-in at the library. We promised we'd go.'

'Are you telling me, Aiza Hassan, that you expect me to release you lot into the community after this – escapade, without even making known to you my thoughts on the matter first?'

'You can make them known tomorrow,' Aiza pleads. 'We won't enjoy ourselves at all, worrying, will we, Dallas?'

Ms O'Leary's mouth twitches.

'All right, love,' says the fireman. The other fireman is on the other side of the railings. Together they lift Ruby up, sliding her swollen knee, both of them climbing up ladders, until they've got her to the cut part – and out. The one on our side brings Ruby down the ladder.

'All right,' says Ms O'Leary. 'I've already spoken to your parents, so just as soon as I've made sure your partner in crime is basically healthy, you can go and fulfil your civic responsibility. But I want all three of you in my office first thing in the morning.'

'I *really* don't want to talk about it,' I say.

'Well tough, I'm afraid. I've held back long enough, hoping you'd come to your senses, but it's clear you need a kick to do that.'

Sam's in a bad mood.

'Come on, you've had long enough to marshal your stupid arguments,' he says. 'I want to hear it. What are you thinking of?'

Jessi's not here so any slight inhibition he may have felt

about slagging her off – and it would only have been slight – is gone.

'She's a forty-one-year-old child. You'll end up living on microwave crap, and cleaning the bathroom, and sitting home alone while she's off chasing men or whatever it is she does in her extensive free time.'

'I won't,' I say. 'She wants to be settled and in a proper house. That's why she wants me.'

'You never said a truer word,' he shouts. 'She wants you for her own selfish pathetic reasons.'

'Don't you think it would be nice, though,' I interrupt. 'To live in a real house. Instead of a two hundred-year-old garage on legs that are stuck into green water?'

'Huh.' He's silent for a second, because this is what he's been saying as long as I can remember. 'I'd like to see what kind of house she can afford on whatever salary she can pull down working in one hospital where they've got time to notice how unreliable she is.'

This is unfair. I'm pretty sure Jessi is a brilliant nurse.

'You'll be sorry in a month. A week. And then where will you be? Texas, that's where.' He throws his hands up in the air. 'Do you reckon Momma would want you doing this?'

That's enough. Something goes *ping* in me. 'I don't CARE,' I shout. 'If Momma would have wanted me living in this SHACK for the whole of my life whether anybody cares about me or not here, she should have bloody well looked where she was going and had her brakes working better, shouldn't she?'

Sam walks out. I see him go jerkily over and pick up his bike and ride off, and I wonder where he goes now, now that he doesn't go to Prue's.

I walk away, to get a drink of water, and lean on the draining board to drink it. The kitchen window is open and outside, with their feet dangling above the water, Violet and Billy are sitting with their backs to me. Violet is talking and they're holding hands.

'It's all right,' she tells me, when they hear me coming and turn around. Billy's crying; at least, he's got tears rolling down his face. I squat down beside him. 'He's just sad because of you going away,' she explains, 'but I'm telling him it's going to be fine.'

I take Billy's other hand. 'I just have to go. For a bit.'

'Why,' says Billy, very quiet.

'I just do.'

Violet stands up, into the river. It's gotten so low it's barely up to her waist. She paddles into it. 'Don't worry, Dallas. I'll look after Billy.'

The sun behind her turns her fluffy hair to gold. 'But who's going to look after you?' I ask.

'Me,' says Billy.

And then Sam appears again, dropping his bike. 'I'm not done with you, Dallas.'

'Don't start in front of them,' I say.

'Oh, you're suddenly so concerned about them? Even though you're choosing to live thousands of miles away?'

'You're leaving too,' I hiss, walking off.

'No I'm not. I'm not leaving.'

'You are, you will. You've been picking out your university since you were my age. Gemma's going to make you go . . .' We're around the back of the boathouse now where I hope Billy can't hear us. 'That's why you want me to stay, so you don't have to feel guilty about going, isn't it? It's got nothing to do with me, or what's best for me, or even Billy. It's you putting it off on me so when you leave . . .'

'I'm not going anywhere,' Sam says through his teeth. 'I'm not going to university because –' and his chin suddenly crumples – 'because I screwed up my exams, OK, and I'm not going to get the grades I need. So it's got nothing to do with that.' He blinks a few times and glares at me. 'I'm going to be here where I'm supposed to be. And if anyone's shoving their guilt off on anyone . . .'

'You screwed up your exams?' I say, bewildered.

'Which exams?' asks Gemma through the window.

Sam blinks again and rubs his nose. 'All of them.'

Later, he cries. I'm trying to look after Billy and Violet at the dinner table while Gemma and Sam talk, but we can all hear him.

'Really truly all of them?' Gemma says. 'I bet you didn't. You've aced every test you've ever done . . .'

'Not these,' Sam says. 'I couldn't answer anything – and I kept thinking the next one would be better. Like you said – it's never happened before.'

'I bet it wasn't as bad as you think.'

Sam laughs. 'It was. And I just got to thinking that this was the way it was meant to be. To make the decision easier – because I was already thinking I couldn't go anyway.' He shrugs and wipes his nose. 'It's a relief. Not to have to think about it.'

Gemma puts her arm across his shoulders. They're both staring ahead of them. 'Why didn't you tell me? Did you tell anyone?'

He shakes his head.

'So if the results come in August and they're as bad as you think,' she says, briskly, 'you'll do retakes.'

'Retakes?'

'Yes. We'll get you a place at the sixth form college if we have to. Don't tell me you'd be embarrassed, Sam. Your mother died in your A-level year, and if that wasn't enough, you've spent virtually all your time since looking after your brother. You'll retake your exams till you get the grades you deserve and then, sometime soon, you'll go off and have a great time at university the way the universe intended. Now, go and wash your face and put a clean T-shirt on.'

'Why?'

Gemma pushes him towards the ladder. 'Because there's a

read-in at our library to attend in twenty minutes, and this time you're coming.'

'Try this,' says Sam, shoving a book into my hands. It's *David Copperfield*.

'What are you trying to do to me?' I ask. The library is much noisier than usual. People actually turned up. Gracie is bustling round trying to make sure everyone has a book.

'Educate you,' he says.

'I've just read *The Outsiders*.' And now I'm reading it again.

'So you're finally on the right path. I won't have you growing up stupid, Dallas. And if you're leaving I don't have long to fix you, do I?'

I take the book.

'How's the knee, Ruby?' Gemma asks.

'It's OK.'

'Let's have a look at it.'

'Honestly, it's OK.'

'Listen, could you do me a favour? Billy wants *Mr Magnolia*, and I've got to go and order the pizza. Could you read it to him?'

'Quite a crowd, Dallas, eh?' Jessi says, handing out iced coffees from a cardboard tray. 'Good atmosphere! What are you reading?'

I show her *David Copperfield*.

'Not bad. The reporter'll like that. Maybe we'd better

start getting everyone shifted around for the photos. Let's get Aiza over here at the table, for a start.'

'Manipulative as ever,' Sam says loudly.

'We need some manipulation,' she says, handing him a coffee. He hands it back. 'The stakes are high. We want to win to honour your mother, don't we, Dallas?'

'Dallas,' Gemma says, 'can I have a word?'

'The photographer's just arrived,' Jessi says.

'He'll be a while setting up.' She pulls me over into the corner behind the counter, where Ruby is reading to Billy.

'I don't want to talk about Texas now,' I say. I mean, this is it. 'This is our last shot.'

'It's nothing about Texas, it's this.' She looks exhausted. 'Listen, Dallas, I know you felt guilty about your mother, and her leaflets. And that got tangled up with this place. But you don't need to feel guilty, it was nothing to do with you, what happened, and she knew you loved her. If this doesn't work – if they shut down the library . . .'

'You don't think we're going to win,' I say.

'It doesn't matter to your mother,' she says. 'I want you to know that she's proud of you either way. She wouldn't . . .'

'She would care,' I say.

'Of course she would, she always did, and do you know how many times she was on the winning side?' Gemma asks. 'She always went in knowing it was fifty to one she would make any sodding difference at all, and that was why she was the bravest woman in the world. I just don't want your heart to be broken over this library, OK?'

'OK,' I say.

'Not that it didn't break her heart every time,' she mutters.

'Ruby,' Gracie says. 'Come here, love, I've a book for you here.'

I look. It's *Geek Girl*. 'You told me not to read that,' I protest. She gives me a look.

'When you were eight. And don't think I didn't see you smuggle it out the same day. Anyway it's a bit of a laugh and a bit of glamour, and don't we all need that these days?'

'Thanks,' says Ruby, taking it. 'Only I don't think I'll have time to read it before – you know.'

Gracie sighs. 'You can take it back to any Oxfordshire library, pet.'

'I don't know where any are,' Ruby says.

The photographer lines us up, moves us around. Takes pictures of people reading, and then all of us crushed together, shouting.

'It'll look good,' says the reporter.

Jessi and Danny and Annie have been on the phone, revving up the council to comment on what's happening and the library still being open now it's seven o'clock. Aiza has opened up a Twitter account just so she can tweet all the newspapers. She keeps taking pictures too. Ruby comes over and hooks her chin over my shoulder to look at Aiza's phone. 'What's that?'

'My new Twitter identity,' Aiza says proudly. 'I'm taking action.'

'Isn't Twitter for old people?'

'Yes, Rubes,' Aiza says. 'That's why you use it to bother old people.'

'I've got to go in a minute,' says Ruby.

'Do you? It's only seven thirty. The pizza's about to arrive.'

'Yeah, I know, but my mum says she's coming to get me.'

'I thought you were at your nan's tonight,' Aiza says.

'Mum had a fight with Paul,' Ruby says, and then doesn't say anything else.

The photographer snaps us, nearly blinding us. It doesn't seem like the best idea to have a picture of us hanging over a phone instead of reading books, but maybe he got *David Copperfield* into shot. It's not bad actually. I might read it properly after I've finished *The Outsiders* again.

And then, just as I'm sinking comfortably into a good scene with Peggotty, a squall breaks out in the picture-book section. Gemma is talking to Gracie. Sam is talking to the reporter. Jessi is talking to a man. I sigh and put my book down.

It's not even Billy. It's Violet, shouting. In a library. Not like her.

'I am a cowboy,' she yells.

'No you're not, no you're not,' a little boy chants. 'You're a girl.'

'So what? I'm a cowgirl then.'

'Cowgirls aren't real,' he says. Little git.

'Yes they are,' she yells. 'My mummy was one.'

The little boy, who has yellow hair I'd like to pull, looks over at Gemma, who looks serious and tidy like she always does on a work day. 'She's not.'

'My other mummy,' says Violet.

Billy hits the little boy on the nose.

'What are you reading, Vi?' I ask, once things have calmed down and the little boy has been removed and given a Kit-Kat by Gracie. I know what she's reading, it's *Little House on the Prairie*, which she's way too young for. 'You know, Momma read us that when I was five.'

She sniffs.

'She loved those books. Sam hated them. Momma got annoyed with him. When she was starting *On the Banks of Plum Creek*, she told him he'd like that one because it was like our life, you know, living by a river, and do you know what he said?'

Violet looks up at me. 'What?'

I grin because I can see Momma now, already frowning because she knew whatever he said it was going to be rude. 'He said the book of our life would be called *On the Banks of Bum Creek*.'

Violet tries desperately hard to look disapproving, but her face cracks and she laughs so hard she snorts. Just like Momma did.

'Ruby!' says Ruby's mum, who appeared scowling at the

door five minutes ago and has been standing by herself watching everyone. 'Come on, we're going *now*.'

'There's going to be pizza,' Ruby says.

'Don't be so greedy. Come on, we're leaving.'

'Mum, I want to stay.'

'Well, you can't. I told you about this, there could be trouble.'

'Just because Paul says . . .'

'It's nothing to do with Paul, Ruby Cox,' her mum snaps. She catches my eye and lowers her voice, but I can still hear. 'Don't you know there can be trouble at things like this? I've told you they're looking for any excuse to take you away, or make you live at your nan's. Is that what you want?'

'No,' Ruby says with a sigh.

Five minutes later and 'Oh my – grief,' says Aiza.

'What?' I ask, looking up from my book *again*. It better be pizza.

Aiza's dad is coming towards us, beaming. There's a woman behind him. 'Oh,' I say.

'Oh no you didn't,' Aiza says to her dad.

'I don't know what that means,' he says. 'I was telling Sofia all about my activist daughter this morning and she wanted to see for herself.'

Aiza's potential new stepmother smiles. She's pretty. Her hair is swishy. She is young.

'Sorry,' Aiza says. 'I've got to see Ruby off. She's leaving.'

She darts away before he can stop her. Sofia laughs. He introduces me to her.

'Nice to meet you, Dallas,' says Sofia. 'What are you reading?'

'*David Copperfield*,' I mumble, showing her.

'Ah. I never read it. Is it good?'

'Pizza!' calls Gemma, bringing in a stack of boxes so high I can't see her face.

'I only came for the pizza,' says Ms O'Leary, appearing at my shoulder.

'You're reading it,' says Sam.

I look up from *David Copperfield* reluctantly and swallow my mouthful of pizza. 'I suppose.'

'Don't drop jalapenos on it.'

'Dallas,' says Gemma, 'we're off.'

'You said we could stay till nine!' I mean, I haven't even had any of the Meat Lover yet.

'Sam will bring you. But the kids are shattered, they need to be in bed.'

'She's coming!'

It's not five minutes since Gemma swept Billy and Violet off, and I'm only on my second slice of Meat Lover. Aiza has just swanned in from nowhere, saying that Ophelia Silk is outside with two sturdy men.

'What? And where have you been?'

She shushes me.

'I thought you'd skipped off home. Your dad went there looking for you.'

'Let him look. Listen, your nemesis is outside. Wipe the sauce off your chin.'

Ophelia Silk sweeps in just then. 'It's just so edifying to see you all here,' she says. Actually there are far fewer people than there were an hour ago. People have been taking their kids home mostly. Her eyes fall on Roger and two of his friends, scoffing the end of the pizza. 'I do so appreciate everything you've all been doing. And perhaps if this library could be this full every morning and every afternoon, things would have been different. But we are where we are, and despite your magnificent efforts, I'm sorry to have to tell you that the library will close on Friday at six o'clock, and it won't reopen.'

There are shouts, and groans, and people are shaking their heads angrily. Aiza hisses. I feel sick. I wish I hadn't eaten so much pizza.

'I know, I know,' Ophelia Silk shouts. 'I'm sad about it too. But come on, now, you can be proud of all you've done. It's just time to let go, that's all. I'm afraid we all have to accept that the Queen Street library has reached the end of its path.'

As if I'm watching a film and it's suddenly slowed down, I see Gracie, standing behind the library counter, behind Ophelia Silk, stand up and pick up a big sloppy piece of cooling pizza from the box on the counter. I see her reach back like a tennis player, with the cheese strands hanging down, and I see her hurl the slice of pizza. My eyes follow it through the air, and I flinch as it splatters against the muted-teal-suited back of Ophelia Silk.

'Bloody hell,' says Aiza, back in real time.

My eyes meet Jessi's. She's standing beside Roger and his friends, with Danny on her other side. Her eyes widen and her face splits in a grin at me. Then she bends over Roger, who has a pizza box on his lap, and she scoops up a slice. Two seconds later it hits Ophelia Silk, who has turned to bellow at Gracie, on the side of the face, and smooshes off on to the floor. I find myself thinking it's a good thing that carpet's probably not going to be used much after this.

Just for a second the library hovers on the edge of absolute carnage. A few more pizza slices get chucked about, and I don't see who's throwing them, because Ms O'Leary has a large graphic novel in each hand and is standing in front of me and Aiza, who's bent in half with giggles. Then Sam pops up beside us, clearly checking to see that we're not amongst the pizza chuckers, and suddenly everything is much calmer and everyone looks awkward. Ophelia Silk, who is going to have to nip into the dry cleaners sometime soon, is wiping her hands on her skirt pockets and ordering her burly men out of the door in front of her.

'Time to leave, I think,' says Ms O'Leary. 'Samuel, I'll rely on you to make sure they get home.' We watch her go, leaving her graphic novels neatly on a low table on her way out.

'Well,' says Sam, 'that was bloody stupid.'

Gracie is sitting, drooping, on a chair. We go over to her.

'Don't worry about it, Gracie,' says Sam.

'I'm so degraded,' she says. 'I'm so humiliated. A woman of my age. How did I start throwing pizza?'

'She's gone now.'

'Thank God. Probably to call the police.'

'She won't call the police,' Sam says. He catches my eye. 'But maybe we'd better head off. Just in case.'

He urges everyone out into the heavy summer rain, including Jessi who's hyperactive and can't stop talking, and once Gracie has locked up and dropped the keys into her big black bag, we all look at each other.

'I'd better take you home, Aiza,' says Sam.

'I'll be fine on my own.'

'Yeah, no. Call your dad and tell him I'm walking you back.'

'I'll come too,' I say.

'No, Dallas,' Sam says. 'You make sure Gracie gets back safe, OK, and then head home with Jessi.'

'You're back earlier than I expected,' says Gemma when we trail in. 'Was it all going well when you left?'

'That – was – hilarious,' says Aiza next morning as we wait in the office. 'Good grief, that was funny. Oh don't look so po-faced, Dallas.'

'The library's shutting.'

'Well, you did what you could. Can I stay at yours tomorrow night by the way?'

I feel a bit doubtful that this is a good idea. My family can't talk about the weather at the moment without having a screaming, roaring fight.

'Please. My dad's got to go to Germany for some emergency meeting and Rabia's got a thing so she can't come round.'

'Well.'

'Seriously, please. You know I can't ask Ruby.'

I do know this. I wouldn't ask to stay at Ruby's myself. I don't even know if her mum would let us, and if she did it would be super weird.

'Dallas, do you know what my dad threatened me with? He said he'd have to ask Sofia if she'd come round and stay over with me. *Just the two of us.*'

'All right,' I say. 'Fine. But don't listen to any words that my family say, right?'

'No problem. I never do. Hi, Rubes. You missed an absolute treat last night.'

Ruby looks tired out, and like she needs to wash her hair. Momma used to say that was a sign of depression, though I don't know if it counts when you're eleven. I mean, I don't usually wash my hair until Sam starts pretending to skid on grease when he walks past me.

She's amazed when we tell her how the read-in turned out. 'You mean there really was a riot?'

222

'I don't know if you'd call it a riot,' I say. 'Bloody waste of pizza was what it was.'

'It was messy,' Aiza agrees.

'Well, what do you know. My mum was right.' Ruby looks all faraway. I'm not sure if she's pleased or not.

Ms O'Leary is surprisingly calm about the whole getting stuck in the fence thing. Maybe it's because the adults at the library and their food fight put it into perspective. We're relieved, especially Ruby. Then we bump into Libby as we're leaving the office.

'Hey, Ruby,' she calls out. 'I heard there was a food fight at the library thing last night. Is that what your mother taught you to do with pizza and books?'

'I'm going to get her,' Ruby mutters. 'I have to get her.'

16

In the morning when Sam rattles on my door and calls, 'Last day!' my eyes fight to get themselves open, as if little fat mice are sitting on my eyelids.

'How do you feel?' Gemma asks at breakfast. 'Emotional?'

'No,' I say. I've been too really sad this year to court fake sadness. 'You won't catch me getting weepy.'

'Some of them will,' Sam says, passing me a plate of toast. 'I know.'

I half wonder, as they wave me off, if anyone will be at the leavers' assembly. I didn't say anything about it, because everyone is busy. I don't mind. It's not that big a deal. We've all three been dying to leave St John's for about three years or something.

Ruby texts that she'll meet us at school, but actually as we turn the last corner we hear her call, and she comes running up with her rucksack bouncing on her back and her cheeks all flushed. 'Where have you been?' Aiza asks.

She puts her finger on her lips, laughs and then bends over with her hands on her knees. 'Stitch,' she wheezes.

'We need to get you fit,' Aiza says. 'And then we need to

get you a bike. Maybe I'll teach you to cycle over the summer – that could be our project. Otherwise who am I going to ride to school with?'

I get a clear picture in my head of Aiza and Ruby cycling to school in autumn – even though I've never seen Ruby on a bike in my life – along the towpath with red and yellow leaves everywhere and me not there.

'Are you all right, Dallas?' asks Ms Wilson.

'Yeah,' I say.

'Are you sure?'

'Of course she is,' says Aiza. 'She's not one of those sobbing saps.'

'I didn't think so,' Ms Wilson agrees. 'Enjoy your last day, girls.'

'What are you up to?' Aiza hisses at Ruby, who's breathing normally again but is being very careful of her backpack.

'I'll tell you in PE.'

Aiza leaps on her and screws her knuckles into Ruby's head. 'Tell us now.'

'It's a secret, OK. I'll tell you in PE.'

I've got a bottle of wine for Mr Chaplin that Gemma bought at the Co-op after I suddenly remembered about needing a present. Ruby doesn't have anything. Aiza has a bottle too, but instead of being wrapped in the wrinkled end of the Christmas paper like mine, it's in a special silver bag. I think it's probably champagne or something. Anyway, he says a lot of nice things to all of us. Then we sit down to listen to Ms O'Leary, who's come into our classroom for the first time all year.

'And I remember what you were like when you started,' she says, beaming round. 'Tiny little things with tidy hair and all wearing clothes much too big for you. Just the opposite of how you are now!'

Everybody laughs, and I think it's a shame she wasted that joke on us when all the parents will be here soon.

'Crying if you saw a man teacher in the corridor, and now look at you! You've survived a whole year of Mr Chaplin!'

We all laugh.

'And seven years of me, which quite frankly . . .'

She goes on for quite a while. 'I was hoping she'd save it all for the parents,' Aiza murmurs, 'my dad deserves to be totally bored. Is Gemma coming, Dallas?'

'No,' I say.

'Nor's my mum,' says Ruby, looking downcast. 'She was going to try and get the morning off. Till she heard my nan was coming.'

Then we have PE. It's not real PE because the kits have gone home, but Mr Chaplin takes us out to play some running round sorts of games. Only Ruby gets a bottle of sun cream out of the front of her bag and starts pouring it all over her arms, while the rest pour out of the cloakroom.

'Do you think I should go out there?' Aiza hisses.

'No. Keep watch,' Ruby says. She runs back into the

classroom, pulling me with her. 'Dallas, help me look at Libby's lunchbox.'

'What?'

'Help me look, so I can put it back right after.' She stares for a few seconds without blinking at Libby's red daisy Cath Kidston lunchbox, and then she puts one hand behind it and shuffles it like she's playing Spillikins. She gets it out without disturbing Sophie's on one side and Zoe's on the other, and then runs back into the cloakroom.

'What are you doing?' I follow.

Ruby has unzipped the box. 'It's Friday,' she says. 'Doughnut day.'

We watch in awe as she extracts an oozy lump. 'Strawberry and cream,' Aiza observes. 'Slumming it today.'

Ruby wraps it in tissue and tucks it into the bottom of Libby's bag, under her pink-piped baseball cap. 'Can't throw it away,' she explains, 'or they'd say I stole it.'

She then takes a white paper package, grease stained, out of her own backpack and carries it over to Libby's lunchbox, and the empty doughnut bag.

'What is that?' Aiza asks.

Ruby folds the paper back. 'I'm not saying,' she says, holding it carefully.

'Why not?'

'I'll tell you after.'

Aiza and I look at each other.

'Seriously, Ruby,' I say, 'it's not anything dangerous is it?'

'Of course not.' She wraps the strawberry-and-cream smeared napkin around it, puts it in the pink striped paper bag and tucks it in between the pot of chopped-up melon and the wrap. 'It's a doughnut.'

'Where did you get it?' Aiza asks.

'My mum,' Ruby says, with a smile.

'She's finishing her crisps.'

'No she isn't. She would never offer Jada the last in the pack.' We watch, trying to look as if the wall display behind them is absolutely fascinating and hasn't been there since we were in Year 3. 'You see, *now* she's finishing them.'

'Don't get excited, she's still got all the iced tea to drink.'

I feel as if my fingers are itching, waiting. We're trying so hard not to make her suspicious – we've already sat down closer than we normally would.

'What is it, what is it, what is it?' Aiza intones, drumming on Ruby's leg under the table.

'Not telling. Just wait.'

We wait.

'If she takes it out of the paper, we're done,' Ruby murmurs.

'Why?'

She shakes her head.

'Oh look!'

Libby's voice cuts through the clamour of the last day of the year in the lunch hall. Ruby goes purple, I'm afraid she might have stopped breathing.

'My absolute favourite, strawberry and cream. Oh God, though, it's just so gooey, I don't think I can eat it without it squirting everywhere. Watch, it's so gooey.'

And everyone watches.

. . . As Libby, her eyes shut now, takes a big bite out of her mostly paper-wrapped treat, and chews.

One second later she blows it out again, all over her lunchbox, and from the way Gilbert Finch falls backwards off the bench opposite, over him too. Then she wails and starts making choking noises.

I nearly choke myself. Aiza has her arms wrapped around her head. 'What was it? Ruby, what was it?'

'A crab doughnut,' Ruby says, slipping under the table.

Aiza howls.

Libby, trying to jump up, gets her foot caught and falls, pulling Jada on top of her. I hear Ruby actually scream with laughter under the table. Sophie catches my eye, and her total confusion makes my chest spasm.

Several teachers congregate at Libby's table.

Naturally we get a telling-off, but it's the last day and there's not much point in making a huge fuss, especially as Ruby is able to tell Ms O'Leary exactly where the original doughnut is, and it's not as if we made her eat something that wasn't food. Ms Wilson mentions in a detached way that crab doughnuts are a proper gourmet dish. To be honest I'm not sure that we'd have got told off at all except that everybody in the hall saw it and it caused a bit of carnage with people laughing so much. And Libby is fuming.

'You'll regret that,' she hisses at Ruby as we leave the office.

'Nah,' Ruby says airily, and asks me in a whisper what regret means.

'That was amazing,' Aiza suddenly says. We're sitting waiting for Mr Chaplin to take the final register, before we go into the hall for the leavers' assembly. She turns to Ruby. 'Ruby, you've made my whole primary school experience worthwhile.'

We look at each other, and all of us burst out laughing. I get snot all over my face.

'My most favourite memory,' Ruby says, holding her paper all squodged up in her fingers, 'is of meeting my friend Dallas, who always used to come to the office with me when I was scared to go on my own, and my friend Aiza, who taught me to like sauce on my food.'

Everyone claps.

'My best memory,' says Aiza, 'is when I came in Year Three and I was expecting everyone to hate me, but most of them were actually OK.' She pauses like a professional comedian for the parents' laugh. 'And most of all I got to be friends with the two people who had the coolest names, Dallas and Ruby, who help me out whenever I need it and never even need to know why.'

Aaaahhh, go the parents, and they clap.

I feel a bit bad after that that my memory is all about tying this girl called Kayla Simms to the fence with my scarf when I was in Year 1 and we were playing a catch game, and then the bell went and I just left her there and went inside and had forgotten all about her three minutes later when the Year 4 teacher came and shouted at me. Which the audience finds funny, like I meant them to, but actually it's a horrible memory and I cried for hours. Anyway. After that Ms O'Leary goes on a bit – I didn't need to worry about her wasting her joke on us, she just tells it again. I sit and look at everybody. I don't know if it's all the laughing I was doing at lunchtime but I can feel tears building up in my cheeks. Even Ruby's mum is there, sitting right at the other side of the hall from Ruby's nan. Aiza's dad is standing at the back, holding his iPad up in the air to record everything. If Momma wasn't dead, she'd be here.

Then I hear a squeal, and I peer back behind all the people who are crowded in the doorway because they turned up too late to get a seat, and I see Billy, climbing all over Sam's head, Gemma shoving a Malteser in his mouth and Jessi eyeballing Gilbert Finch's dad.

It's time for us to go up one by one and get our certificates from Ms O'Leary. The parents clap enthusiastically, but when it's my turn my family scream and whoop and shriek, every one of them.

'I thought you weren't coming,' I say afterwards.

'Wouldn't have missed it,' Gemma says. 'But I've got to dash off and get Violet now because they've got some songs and – she was sorry not to be here. We'll see you at home. You too, Aiza,' because Aiza's dad is just leaving for the airport.

Jessi has a hot date in London, or so she says. She takes a selfie of me and her, me holding my certificate, for Granma, and kisses me on the cheek. 'I'm real proud of you,' she says. 'You made it.'

I watch them all go. I wish I could stop thinking about leaving. The decision's made, I've upset everyone and they're beginning to get over it, just like the decision's been made on the library and all that's left to do is get over it. I've had a lot of practice lately, getting over things. We all have. I ought to be better at it by now.

'What's wrong with your family?' Aiza asks me after dinner, which has been fairly sullen, as though they all used up all the good temper on being nice in assembly earlier. We're sitting outside on the bank, dipping our toes in the lazy river.

'They're all hacked off with me about going to Texas.'

Aiza looks at me for a while in silence. I carry on picking daisies. 'Are you really going?' she asks in the end.

'Yeah,' I say.

There's a silence, and I look up. Aiza is gazing past me, towards the towpath. It's so still tonight you can hear the runners grunting and the boaties calling to each other.

'Yeah,' she finally says. 'I can see it would upset them.'

Gemma leaves Sam to put the kids to bed, because she wants to go and see Gracie. I don't want to think about it – the library shut forever. I'm over the losing part, I don't think this is just crushed ego or even disappointment. But I don't want to think about the library.

'We should be celebrating,' Aiza says, so we put *Pitch Perfect* on the laptop and get the chocolate digestives out.

'What a shame we're too young for champagne,' I say.

'I wonder if Ruby's OK,' Aiza says. We asked her to come round too, but her nan was taking her and her mum out for fish and chips, and Ruby was all hopeful that it would mean they'd make up properly and stop fighting.

'*Pitch Perfect* again? Really?' Sam asks, and sits down next to us to watch it.

'*Pitch Perfect* again?' Gemma asks, coming in later. She sounds tired. I pause the film and look up.

'How's Gracie?'

She shrugs. 'Well into the whisky. Danny and Annie have got her on their boat, and they said they'd keep her tonight if she has a couple too many.' She pats me on the head. 'She'll be all right. In a while.'

* * *

Normally when Aiza sleeps over we talk for hours. But tonight – maybe she's tired too.

'I love your room,' she says, before I turn out the light.

'It's hardly a room.'

'I know – but it's better. It's like a nest.'

I switch off the light, and push the window further open.

I've got used to bad nights every now and again, over the last year, but this one isn't about Momma. I'm not afraid of my chest bursting with pain, I'm not even crying. I just – it's as if everything that's happened has piled up in my head, and it stops me sleeping. I think about acceptance. That line about knowing the difference between the things you can't change and the things you can. I think about the library, and I think about where I live. And where I want to live.

It's not even that late when I come to my decisions.

'Aiza,' I hiss.

'Mmmff.'

'Aiza, shut up. And wake up.'

'Why? It's still dark.' She rolls over and squints at me. 'Are you wearing clothes?'

'Yes. You need to get up and get dressed.'

She groans, but she sits up. 'Are we having an adventure or something?'

17

We get out of the window. We used to do it all the time; we only stopped so Billy and Violet wouldn't start copying us. They're asleep now. All you have to do is drop on to the downstairs roof and creep to the edge. Then there are lots of toeholds in the bricks. That's the beauty of them being so old. But we have to be quiet. 'And it's dark,' Aiza points out.

'There's all that moonlight. I'll go first if you want.'

'Yeah you will.'

I'd be fine, except just as I'm poised on the edge Lonesome brushes up against me and nearly gives me a heart attack. Then, when I'm clinging to the guttering trying to find my next toehold, he sticks his nose in my ear and climbs down me, over my shoulder and all the way down my back. Aiza clambers past me. 'Come on, Dallas,' she says.

The river is very quiet. We're far enough from any road not to get any sound lower than a police-car siren. All you can hear is the scrunch of our feet, and an occasional bird, and the lapping of the water against the boats.

Gracie's gangplank is out, but I know it squeaks. I go across it on my belly so I can hold it still as I get on deck, and pray that none of the dogs along this stretch are awake right now.

She really ought to lock her door.

I don't dare to use even the light of my phone, but the curtains are thin and when I've stood still for a minute there's enough light to move around by. I get Gracie's bag, hanging up where it always is, and cradle it in case it jangles.

'Did you get 'em?' Aiza hisses as I sit down on the gangplank and turn carefully over on to my belly. I don't shush her. That shhh sound would probably wake the dogs. But as I kneel and then stand back up on the towpath I seize her hand and pull her away, so fast she nearly trips.

'Did you get 'em?'

I show her the keys. 'Now be quiet.'

'I am being quiet. Ruby's going to meet us outside her building.'

We're past the boats now. 'I said not to text Ruby till I had the keys.'

'Well, once you were on the boat it was obvious you were going to get them.'

I laugh at her. 'You know I didn't tell you this, but Gracie has a gun on that boat.'

'A what now?'

'A gun.'

'She does not.'

'In case of intruders. Now come on.'

She follows me with her mouth open, until a midge flies into it. I don't tell her it's an air rifle. It's good for Aiza to feel challenged once in a while. Ruby's waiting for us – I can see her pink hoodie a mile off in the moonlight. 'I thought you'd given up,' she says to me.

'I had.'

She grins.

We take our time. There's no rush, and the air – it's like swimming, tonight. The moon is painted on the sky like a lemon slice. 'I can't believe we're doing this,' Aiza says. 'Are we going to get into trouble?'

'Nah,' Ruby says. 'We're eleven.'

'One of these days that's going to stop working,' Aiza says.

'Yeah. Like when we're twelve.'

We cut across the corner of the meadow, to avoid going back past the boats. The grass is almost up to my knees, and soaks my trainers. It's like paddling, but more swishy. 'Good thing I didn't put my new shoes on,' Aiza says, and trips. She grabs at both of us and pulls Ruby over. I manage to land on my knees.

A flock of lapwings takes off at the edge of the grass, in a diagonal line so sharp it looks like it's been drawn with a ruler. They cry in protest at being disturbed so early. I kneel on the wriggling, giggling heap that's my friends, and watch them fly away, low over the river.

'It's early for lapwings,' I say as we walk up Queen Street.

'It's early for everything,' says Ruby, yawning so wide her eyes disappear.

Queen Street is darker than it was by the river or in the

meadow, and there's nobody around except us. We draw closer together. Ruby has hold of the cuff of my hoodie. Then it takes us a while to get the door open; the lock's stiff.

'What if there's a burglar alarm?' Ruby asks, holding on to my cuff to stop my turning the handle.

'Of course there's a burglar alarm,' I say, pulling the door open. 'Get in and shut the door.'

'There's a burglar alarm?' Aiza says, her head turning this way and that as if she's expecting to see red laser beams like in *Mission Impossible* or something.

'It's all right,' I say, walking over to it. 'I know the code.'

We don't turn the light on, we just open the blinds at the back. The sky is already much lighter, and we can see well enough to move around.

'I want to read,' Aiza says.

'No you don't,' I tell her. 'You want to sleep. It could be a long day tomorrow. Lots of reading time then.'

She yawns. 'You're boring for an outlaw, Dallas.'

And then we all settle down.

'I'm starving,' Ruby says much later. I jump; I thought she was asleep.

'You had fish and chips for dinner,' says Aiza's voice from the floor.

'So?'

'So you should be stuffed.'

'Well. I'm not.'

'How did your mum and your nan get on?'

There's a silence. I turn on to my side. I can see Ruby's profile. 'The same. I don't know why they can't be nice to each other.' She goes silent again. 'I'd do anything if they would.'

'I know,' I say.

'You're lucky, Aiza,' she says suddenly. 'It's you who makes all the trouble in your family, so you can stop any time you want.'

There's a silence while Aiza gapes.

'Me?'

'Yeah, of course you. It's just you and your dad, so it's all up to you.'

'Yeah, until he brings this rinky-dink girlfriend into the picture.'

Ruby sighs. 'If your dad's found a nice girlfriend, what's the problem?'

'She's not a nice girlfriend.'

'You don't know that, Aiza,' I point out.

'Exactly,' Ruby says. 'And you're not going to find out as long as you keep running off every time she shows her face. Why do you do that?'

'I don't want a stepmother,' Aiza mumbles.

'Why not?' Ruby sounds fed up. 'A stepmother might be fantastic. Look at Dallas and Gemma.'

'Gemma's OK,' I admit.

'Just exactly what do you think would have happened to Dallas, and Billy, if they hadn't of had a stepmother?' Ruby asks Aiza, sounding like a lawyer off TV.

'Well,' I protest, 'we have got Jessi.'

'Yeah, you do now. But Jessi hasn't been here for the last nine months or whatever, has she? She's been off.'

'She had to finish her job!'

'Yeah, Dallas, that's what I mean.' She rolls over on her side. I can't see her face but I know she's looking in my direction. 'So where do you reckon you would have been for the last nine months, you and Billy? In care, that's where. Or in Scotland. With your dad.'

'Sam . . .'

'Sam's only just turned eighteen, they wouldn't have let him look after you. And even now, it's only you that Jessi's taking, isn't it? So Billy, he'd still be in care. If it wasn't for Gemma. You see what I mean, Aiza?'

'Oh shut up.'

There's another long pause.

'I asked my dad about my mum,' Aiza says. 'Why she left. If it was about me.'

I sit up and nearly fall on top of her.

'All right, Dallas, I'm not so emotional I need you to flatten me,' she says, pushing me back on to the sofa. 'It was OK. We had a good talk, sort of. He said it wasn't about me at all. I feel OK about it now.'

Ruby snuffles.

'Oh, Rubes, don't get slushy.' She turns over. 'Anyway it got me out of trouble after the read-in when I ran off. And made Dad feel guilty about having to go to Germany this week.' There's a massive yawn. 'He'll be bringing me back a huge present.'

By the time the sky gets past bright and into daytime blue, my face has that all-night feel again. I'm lying on one of the sofas squinting up at the skylight, pretending to be asleep but really I'm waiting for something to happen. Ruby is curled up on the other sofa, across from me. Aiza has hauled all the giant beanbags out of the picture-book section and made a nest, all I can see of her is one shoulder and a plait.

I don't know what I'm expecting.

I mean, it's Saturday, and I had a friend sleeping over last night, so it could be late before anybody busts into my bedroom . . . I don't know how late Ruby normally sleeps in. We could be here for a long time. My stomach rumbles – just as if I didn't eat loads of biscuits last night.

I lie, and squint. And think.

A cloud floats above me. I watch it on its way.

Somebody pounds on the door.

18

'Shhh,' Aiza hisses, her head sticking up out of the beanbags.

Ruby gallops to the edge of the romance shelf, and peers out cautiously.

'Do you think it's the police?' Aiza mouths at me. I shake my head so violently I give myself a headache. 'Why not? What time is it?'

'Ten to seven,' I whisper back. 'They won't have found out we're missing yet.'

'They might have done.'

Ruby's voice makes us jump. 'It's the postman.'

'I thought it was all over,' I say, putting the 'We Missed You' Royal Mail card on the counter.

Aiza yawns. 'I'm starving.'

'You better go back to sleep then because there's nothing to eat,' Ruby says. She's got the fridge door open.

'No,' I say, 'you can't go back to sleep. It's campaign time.'

Aiza draws a massive sign – 'THIS IS OUR LIBRARY' – and while Ruby colours it in with the least worn-out pens we can find, she starts tweeting.

'Reporters first,' I say.

'What am I saying?'

'"Children occupying Queen Street library?"' I suggest.

'I don't know if that's going to catch anyone's eye.'

I consider this. 'What about "Children illegally occupying Queen Street library"?'

'Do we know for sure it's illegal?'

'Aiza, I broke into somebody's boat and stole their keys so we could get in. I'm fairly sure it's illegal.'

'Well, yeah, but if we're the ones who say it first, then we're admitting that we know it's illegal, so we won't be able to say we did it in blissful childish ignorance, will we? Plausible deniability, Dallas. You don't watch enough TV, that's your problem.'

We look at each other, and then I have a stroke of genius and take her phone off her. She watches as I tap in:

Children "illegally" occupying Queen Street library

'OK, brilliant,' Aiza says, and taking her phone back she adds on: *in attempt to save it from council budget slashes*

'We're doing her job for her,' I say. 'All she's got to do is cut and paste.'

We retweet it, at the BBC and BBC Oxford, and the *Guardian*, and the *Mail*, and the *Mirror*. I won't let Aiza send it to the *Sun*. 'We've got to have some standards.'

'Oh,' she says, 'good point,' and tweets it at the *Evening Standard*.

Then she starts doing the internet news outlets, and I help Ruby colour in. The sign looks pretty good. And as long as we're all talking and doing stuff, none of us go on too much about how hungry we are.

At eight o'clock, just as we're considering how to attach our poster to the window, the door goes again.

'Now who could that be?' I say.

'The Big Bad Wolf?' Aiza suggests. 'Well, it's time we stopped hiding, considering that as soon as any of these lazy journalists wake up and look at their phones . . .' She marches up to the window and looks out. 'Oh.' She turns round. 'It's your mum, Ruby.'

Ruby's mum comes in without shouting. In fact her eyes light up when I open the door and even more when she sees Ruby. She's holding a tin-foil cube.

'How did you know we were here?' Aiza asks her.

'I left a note,' Ruby says.

'Ruby!'

'Well! You're texting the whole world telling them we're here, aren't you? I didn't mean for you to come out, Mum.'

'Well, here I am,' says Ruby's mum.

'Are you going to stay?' Aiza says doubtfully. We look at each other.

'The more the merrier?' I say.

'Ruby, I never said much all the other times, not even when it was all of you getting lost in London,' Ruby's mum says. 'But I told you the other night – you could get yourself into trouble, doing this.'

'I don't care,' says Ruby. 'It's worth it.'

'Then best we're in it together. At least then they can't say I don't know where you are. I won't be in the way,' she says. 'I brought some toast.'

'What does Paul say?' Ruby asks, holding up her hand to stop me and Aiza falling on the tin-foil cube. She looks stern.

Her mum sniffs. 'Paul's working in Kidlington today. Anyway, he's not the boss of me, is he? Come on, Ruby, find a plate for this. Dallas and Aiza look like they're about to bite my hands off.'

Naturally the toast is stone-cold, leathery round the edges and soggy in the middle, but we all scoff it. Ruby's mum sits down at the low table and starts reading yesterday's paper. I suddenly feel like everything's quite normal. Well, part of me does, and it goes to war in my stomach with the part that says I should have left a note too.

Then I go to the bathroom and find that my period has started. I mean, seriously. It's like a joke. It wouldn't even matter if only there was a reasonable supply of toilet paper, but Gracie must have been letting it run down. When I come back I've got three missed calls from Gemma. I try and call back but it goes straight to answerphone, so I leave a sheepish message.

At twenty-five past eight the door rattles again, this time as if an elephant is trying to headbutt it out of the way.

'Oh my God,' says Ruby's mum.

'It's all right,' Aiza says, squinting between the posters that are stuck to the door. 'It's only Gracie.'

Of course Gracie happens to be the adult I burgled in the middle of last night, but actually she thinks it's fairly brilliant, once she's grasped what's going on. 'Glory be to God,' she says, sinking down opposite Ruby's mum. 'You put the heart across me, Dallas. I thought I'd lost the keys and all the computers would have been robbed and they'd have me arrested for sabotage. And here it's only you three, exercising your civic duties again.'

'Our civic duties are well exercised,' I agree.

'Isn't it a shame there's no milk for tea? If I'd have known I'd have left it last night. And I'm going to have an eye-buster of a hangover in about half an hour's time.'

'Have a lie-down,' Ruby's mum suggests.

'I might.' She puts her feet up. 'Did you start that book yet, Ruby?'

'Yeah,' Ruby says. 'I've got it here. It's funny.'

'That's grand. I've the sequels over on the shelf, I'll fix you up with them later.'

A few minutes later I get a text. Jessi.

Where r u

Library I text back. No point hiding it now. And Jessi's not in Oxford so I've got time before she can get here.

I knew it on my way

I hesitate, then I text back.

Can you bring me some sanitary pads

A minute's pause, then:

!!!!!!!!!

'Jaysus, this hangover's going to be a killer,' Gracie says.

'Just lie back and keep your eyes shut,' Ruby's mum advises.

Gracie sits up. 'Will I go out and buy us a round of bacon sandwiches?'

'No,' Aiza cries. 'Look, it's all right if you want to stay.'

'Good of you, darling,' Gracie says, raising one eyebrow.

'It was meant to be just us kids, but if you lot want to risk getting grief for being here illegally, whatever. But we can't keep opening and shutting the door, all right? It's locked now and it's got to stay locked.'

She biffs the door to make her point, a split second before someone hits it from the other side, so hard that her hand bounces off it. 'Dallas,' the someone howls.

We all look at each other.

Aiza unlocks the door, and jumps back just in time not to get hit in the face as it flies open. Gemma bowls in, holding Billy in her arms and with Violet hanging on to her shirt tail.

So apparently it was criminally irresponsible of me to do this, involving a guest for whom Gemma was responsible, and we could have been killed getting off the roof, and who do I think I am breaking into somebody else's home, and do I realise what I've done, and what the hell do I think I'm doing?

Ruby puts the kettle on.

'We don't have any milk,' Aiza hisses at her.

Oh, so we've done this without even making any proper preparations, well that's just typical, and when am I going to grow up and stop being so whimsical, and do I realise that the last two hours have been some of the worst of Gemma's life, and Sam is out risking his life cycling on flat tyres around Oxford at the speed of light to try and find me?

'I'm sorry,' I say. 'Do you want me to call him?'

'Well, I think someone had better.' She stands and looks at me for a minute with her hands on her hips. 'And I suppose I'd better go and get some food.'

'You can't,' Aiza says, and wilts as Gemma turns towards her. 'I mean, we're meant to be – the police or something could turn up any minute. We've been tweeting . . . I mean, we ought to keep the door shut.'

'Certainly,' Gemma says. 'But since discovering you two beauties were missing, I haven't had any breakfast, and neither have these four-year-olds. Besides, how long do you think your siege is going to last if you don't have any food?'

'Siege?' Aiza mutters to me.

I follow Gemma towards the door.

'I'm coming back,' she tells me. 'And I need you to keep an eye on Billy and Violet.'

'I know,' I say. 'It's just . . .'

'What? What is it?'

I reach up to whisper in her ear. 'Could you get some sanitary towels?'

'What?'

I roll my eyes.

'Are you serious?'

'Yes.'

'Since when?'

'Well . . . oh, I see. This is the second.'

'Dallas Kelly. You are such a monster.' She flings her arms round me, squeezes me breathless and then flies out of the door. 'Lock it behind me.'

'And what if the police are outside when you get back?' Aiza calls after her.

'I'd like to see them get in my way,' Gemma shouts over her shoulder. She's only been gone five minutes when Sam turns up.

'God, you're such a set of drama queens,' he says.

'We,' Ruby says severely, 'are trying to save the library.'

'Yeah, but do you have to be such show-offs about it?' He sits down and picks up a paper.

Aiza squeaks. 'Look! The eagle has landed!'

'What eagle?' Ruby says.

Aiza holds out her phone, then, as we all rush towards it and bang into each other, she turns it back to herself and reads out loud: '"Queen Street library, closed yesterday apparently forever, has been occupied by a group of defiant local schoolchildren. The council are unavailable for comment."'

We all look at each other.

'Wait! Here's another! "Can children save Queen Street library from maw of Tory cuts?"'

'"Maw"?' Ruby says.

'Oh, I like that.' She types furiously. 'Hashtagtorymaw, that's beautiful.'

'We need our own hashtag,' Sam says.

'We've got one, dopey,' Aiza says. 'Queenstlibraryforever.'

'Not very original,' says Sam.

'Nice and simple,' I say.

Gemma kicks the door and hollers. When we let her in she's got about fifty bags full of stuff. 'The garrison is now a bit more provisioned. Stick the kettle on, somebody.'

'We're practically trending,' says Aiza.

'You've had two retweets,' says Sam.

'Look!' Ruby says, hanging over Aiza's shoulder. 'Other libraries are tweeting about us!'

'Oh yeah. Look at that. Macclesfield library – and Taunton . . . Some Scottish one has used the hashtag!'

'Didn't I tell you librarians were the best?' Gracie says smugly.

I go off to make the tea, since everyone's busy.

'Gemma,' I say.

She's sitting on the purple beanbag with Billy between

her legs, reading *Mog* in Polish while he devours a pain au chocolat. I hand her a mug of tea.

'Thanks, pet.'

'I'm sorry about running off and not telling you.'

'I know you are.'

I hesitate, then I sit down *plunk* on the floor next to them. She sips the tea.

'Dallas, you should have told me about your period starting. No, it's probably my fault. Sam never told me about his exams either. I feel like I've been letting everyone down.'

'We did tell you in the end.'

'Yeah. Well.'

'Gemma. Is it OK if I – after all – if I stay?'

She puts her mug down carefully underneath the radiator before she looks at me. 'Are you sure?'

'Yeah.' I take a swallow of her tea out of embarrassment, while she wipes her eyes.

'Why do you want to stay?' she asks me then. What I want to do is shrug it off, but I try and answer, because I think I ought to.

'This is my family,' I say in the end. I wave my arm, at her and Sam and Billy and Violet, and Aiza and Ruby, and Gracie too. 'I mean – Jessi is, of course. But it's different. I belong . . . here.'

She reaches across and tousles my hair. 'Have you told Jessi?'

I shake my head.

She looks at me for a minute. 'Do you want me to do it? I could say I won't let you go, if you want. It might make it easier on her as well as on you.'

I shake my head again. I know what she means but I don't want to be telling lies that could last for years.

'Listen,' she says. 'There are going to be some changes.'

'OK.'

'No more running off. No more living at Aiza's. If you want to see Aiza and Ruby so much, they can come round to our house. And as for you,' she says to Sam who's lounged across to us, 'you are going to take a proper amount of time for yourself and for your homework and occasionally even to see a friend or two, all right? No, no arguing. The only reason Billy depends on you so much is that you haven't let him learn to depend on me. What is it, you still think I don't love him as much as you do?'

'Well,' Sam says, 'we can talk about it another time.'

'Of course we can,' Gemma says. 'As long as it's understood that you're going to do what I say. Now, Billy, why don't we see if we can find that Gujurati *Peepo* that you like so much?'

'What was that about?' Sam asks, when she's gone off to the picture-book section.

'I told her I want to stay. And it's not because you told me to, either.'

He swallows, and then he grins. 'I'm glad,' he says.

'Yeah. Well. Good.'

'So why did you change your mind, if it wasn't my excellent and well-reasoned arguments?'

I shrug. I look round the library at everyone tweeting and tea-drinking and reading. 'This is where I want to be,' I say.

'The council are still speechless,' Aiza says, her brow all furrowed as she flicks through Twitter. 'But some ordinary people are retweeting us – oh good grief.'

'What?'

'Mr Chaplin just used our hashtag.'

'Oh no.'

'It's like that time that Ms O'Leary dabbed in assembly.'

There's a polite knock at the door.

'Who is it?' Aiza yells.

'It's the police,' a nice voice calls back. 'Can I talk to whoever's in charge?'

Everyone looks at me.

'Sure,' I yell back.

'You know that you're not supposed to be in there, don't you?'

'It's public property,' I yell. Gracie gives me a thumbs up. There's a pause.

'Are there any adults in there with you?'

I look doubtfully from Gracie to Ruby's mum to Sam to Gemma.

'Yes,' Gemma calls.

'Good. As long as you're not unsupervised, I can leave you

alone for a bit.' We hear her laugh. 'Have you all got something to read?'

'It's really taking off,' Aiza says half an hour later. 'Look at this. Someone tweeted a picture of the police outside.'

'When you say someone . . .'

'OK, it was me, but someone else has retweeted it.'

There's another knock at the door.

'Is that the police?' Ruby calls, being closest.

Pause.

'Er . . . no. It's . . . er, it's Sofia.'

Aiza shoves Ruby aside at the door. 'What are you doing here?'

'Your dad asked me to come and make sure you're OK, Aiza.'

'I had to tell him where you were,' Gemma says mildly when Aiza glares at her.

'You can tell him I'm fine,' Aiza calls.

'I'd like to see you first.'

'I can't let you in.'

Pause.

'Why not?'

'I can't open the door, the police are out there.'

'They're standing back. Honestly. Look out of the window if you don't believe me.'

Eventually Gemma and Sam make Aiza open the door, and Sofia comes in. 'Well,' she says. 'This is more interesting than my usual Saturday morning.'

Endless cups of tea means that there is a perpetual queue for the loo.

'If they want to get us out of here,' Sam murmurs, 'all they need to do is shut off the water so we can't flush. We'd be done in five minutes.'

A while later Aiza screeches, and because she's been sulking her head off since Sofia got here, we all jump.

'It's the big one!'

'What?'

'The BBC have retweeted us!'

And they genuinely have. The actual BBC have used our hashtag.

'Wow,' I say.

'That's pretty good,' Sam says.

'Let's see what your one at the council says now,' Gracie says.

The door goes again. Whoever it is doesn't stop banging on it till Sam has it all the way open.

'Thanks, nephew,' says Jessi as she breezes in. She's got a million bags as well, which she hands to Sam before she yanks me, Aiza and Ruby into a group hug. 'How are my brave imaginative campaigners?'

'Hungry,' says Ruby, following Sam and the bags into the kitchen.

'You can't be hungry again, Ruby,' says Aiza, 'you've just eaten about six pastries and two bags of Wotsits.'

'Reading makes me hungry.'

I look at Jessi. 'Can I talk to you?'

We sit outside, on the back terrace. It's just a tiny square of garden with one table in it. Aiza's decided a SWAT team isn't likely to come swarming over the back wall, and that it's therefore safe for us to sit out here for a few minutes. I throw a bit of my sandwich to a sparrow. 'I can't go to Texas.'

She doesn't fall down in shock, or anything. She doesn't even say a word. She just pulls on her cigarette.

'Part of me wants to, and everything. But I can't leave – I can't leave Billy and Sam. Or Gemma and Violet. They need me, I mean.' She doesn't say anything and I burble on. 'Momma once said, about Dad leaving, nobody should stay just out of guilt, but I don't think she really meant it. She just knew it would be easier on us all, actually, if . . .'

Quite suddenly she presses her forearm to her eyes and holds it there. I stop talking. She rubs her nose with her other hand. 'I need you too.'

I know she does. I suppose it's nice to be needed but it can tear you in two. And it's more than that anyway – because they'd get by without me if they had to. But I don't want them to have to. And I belong here. When I think of going to Texas with her there's so much that might be great, but it isn't right all the same. I don't know how to put into words what I mean. 'I can't be Momma.'

'Who's asking you to?'

'You are. You want me to come and live with you so you'll

feel like you've got Momma back. And I thought you would be her, for me. But we can't be. Either of us.'

She flicks her cigarette on to the moss and crushes it. 'It's the closest we're going to get.'

I rest my forehead on her shoulder. 'There isn't any closest.' She turns, finally. 'I can't have her. You can't have her. She's gone. But I've still got the rest of my family. And they all love me.'

'I love you.'

'I know you do. And I love you. You're still my favourite auntie.'

She scrabbles in her cigarette pack. 'So what am I going to do, all on my own?'

I strike a match for her and hold it to the end of her cigarette. One of these days I'll have to start nagging her to quit, but not today. 'Get a cat, like you said. A dog, even. Come see us a lot. You'll be all right. You're tough.'

She puts her hand up to her eyes to block out the sun. 'I never really thought you'd come. You're too damn like your momma, Dallas Kelly.'

I put my hand out, and she takes it.

'Dallas!' Ruby shouts as we go back in. 'The council are preparing their response!'

'What?'

'Our pet reporter,' Aiza says. 'She's got a rolling piece – minute by minute, Dallas – on the *Oxford Times* website and there's a link to it on the *Guardian* webpage.'

'Media storm,' says Sam as I walk into the kitchen.

'Yes,' I say, surveying the table. We've got enough bread and sanitary towels to live in here for a year.

'I'm glad you did this,' he says. 'And I am glad you're staying.'

Violet's head snaps round towards me. 'You're staying?'

'Yes.'

'You're not going to Texas?'

'No, I'm staying.'

She looks round, then picks up a packet of four Mars bars and offers it to me.

'Billy,' Gemma says, when I go back out. He doesn't look up from Violet's Tintin book, where he's tracing all the different book covers with his finger.

'Billy, Dallas is staying.'

He looks up.

'She's not going to go to Texas. She's going to stay with us.'

'I know,' he says, getting up. He picks up the Tintin book and plonks himself down in my lap to look at it again.

'What's she up to?' Gracie asks, stopping her nervous pacing to stand beside Aiza, who hasn't looked up from her phone in about two hours.

'I don't know. They should have been able to get some kind of comment out of her by now. I mean, the street is full of reporters and photographers.'

Full is an overstatement, but there are probably about four. And about four police too. I stretch up over our poster to have another look.

'Oh,' I say.

'What?'

'Ophelia Silk just got out of a car.'

There's a crush around the window, until Aiza orders us away. 'A bit of dignity, please, people. We don't want the leading photograph to be us wetting our knickers over the council leader being here, do we.'

'I'm nervous,' Ruby says. 'What if she comes in with her bouncers?'

'That would be – brilliant,' Aiza says. 'I trust everybody's ready to start filming in case they try an invasion?'

'I feel like I want to chain myself to the bookshelves,' Ruby's mum says.

'I could go and get the steering lock off the Porsche,' Sofia offers.

Aiza's eyes narrow. 'What are you doing driving my dad's car?'

'I'm not,' Sofia says. 'I wouldn't be seen dead in that red monstrosity. Mine's a classy blue.'

'You've got a Porsche?'

'I'm glad you're not hung up on worldly details, Aiza,' Gemma says.

There's a knock at the door. Everyone gathers around it to listen.

'I thought we'd got all this sorted, Dallas,' Ophelia Silk says through the door. I don't respond. 'Can we talk?'

'You can't come in,' I say.

'Will you come out?'

I look round, at Aiza who's shaking her head, and Ruby and Ruby's mum who's holding her hand. I look from Gemma to Jessi, and at Gracie who's sitting down with Violet on her lap for ballast, and Billy's who's lying on his back surrounded by Tintin books. I catch Sam's eye.

'Sure,' I say.

When I step outside, blinking, there's an actual clamour. Four different reporters start shouting questions at me.

'How long have you been in there, Dallas?'

'How long are you planning to stay?'

'Whose idea was it, Dallas?'

'What do you want to tell our readers, Dallas?'

'You've created quite a stir,' Ophelia Silk says to me out of the side of her mouth.

'I just want to make a statement,' I say to the reporters, 'so that people know we're not doing this for a laugh or just to be annoying. We want to save this library. People use it, and they deserve it. Libraries are what make people in this country equal, they're about all that make them equal these days. I know the council doesn't have much money, but this isn't a luxury. We need this. You know?'

'But the library's closed,' a reporter calls. 'Do you think you can change that?'

I look at him. I don't look at Ophelia Silk, standing beside me. 'Somebody told me that sometimes you have to accept things. And I know that's true. But this isn't one of those times. I don't have to accept this. And I'm not going to accept it.'

There's a massive cheer from inside the library and – weirdly – one from across the street as well. There's a small crowd of people, mostly mothers and fathers with pushchairs, watching us.

'That's all I have to say,' I finish, and I step back inside.

'Oh good grief on a – what the – hey, Dallas!' Aiza says half an hour later. 'You're viral!'

And I have to watch myself give that statement, all awkward and sweaty, beamed out of Aiza's phone from several different news outlets.

'What'll we do for dinner?' Gemma asks later.

Sam groans. 'If I eat any more bread I might actually die of some gut-twisting over-extension.'

'Chinese it is.'

'I guess we're ordering in,' Jessi says and they laugh.

'Unless we're home by then,' Gemma says. 'Jessi, you'll join us if we are, won't you?'

Jessi grins at me. 'I'd love to.'

'OK,' Aiza says. 'OK, this might be it.'

'What might be?'

'They're gearing up for a live statement from the head of

the council, right outside Queen Street. Aaaaaah, this is too exciting.'

Everyone clusters like flies on honey around Aiza and her phone, except for me. I amble towards the door and push it open.

Ophelia Silk is standing outside, with a big tough bodyguard-style man on one side of her and a lovely kind-looking lady on the other. All bases covered.

'In the light of the passion we've seen here today, and over the last few weeks,' she says, 'and I'm not dwelling upon the illegal aspect of today's occupation because none of us want to look hardly upon the idealism of children . . .'

'Oh, get on with it,' says Gracie.

'. . . in the light of the support this library has in all sections of our community, and because I am not a leader who refuses to listen, or to re-examine decisions when circumstances change . . .'

'Mother of God, will you spit it out?'

'. . . because of all of these things, I am happy to announce this afternoon that the decision to shut down Queen Street library is going to be re-examined.'

The reporters all start shouting. She holds up her hand.

'I can't make promises about the nature of this library's future. But I am happy to promise that it has one.'

The crowd – inside and outside the library – goes nuts.

Ophelia Silk walks over to me. She holds out her hand.

When I take it, she puts her other arm round me and turns me to face the cameras.

'Well done, Dallas,' she says under her breath.

'Thanks,' I say, pulling a grin for the front pages.

'I'm looking forward to seeing you again some time. Maybe around the next election.'

'I'll be on the other side,' I say, turning and grinning in a different direction.

'Oh, I'm sure of it,' she says, and lets go of me, walking off towards her car and waving all the way.

19

'We did it!'

Aiza is doing somersaults all down Queen Street.

'Don't get too cocky,' Sofia advises her. 'Your father is itching to have a few words with you once his meeting is over.'

'Oh, Dad will understand when I explain it to him,' Aiza says, upside down. 'He always does.'

Sofia sighs. 'Yes, I'm sure he does.'

'WE DID IT!' Aiza yells at the sky, and dances off down the street. Ruby and I trudge after her.

'Are you pleased?' Ruby asks me.

'Of course I am.'

'Good.'

'Listen,' I say. 'I'm not going to Texas. I'm staying right here.'

Ruby stops dead and looks at me. Her bottom lip trembles. 'Really?'

'Yeah, I'm staying. Can't leave the library, can I? No – Ruby – don't cry. I'm joking about the library, but I am staying. Going to the new school with you in September. The whole bit.'

Aiza, dancing back, hears this, and jumps on top of me

like a footballer after a goal. I go down, just avoiding splitting my head open on the kerb. Ruby hesitates, then jumps on top of us.

'Are you sure you won't come back to our place?' Gemma asks Sofia and Ruby's mum, over our heads. 'There's loads we could knock into a meal.'

'Thank you,' Sofia says, 'but I think Aiza needs to calm down a bit and spend some time with me. And her dad. Over Skype.'

Aiza groans into my ear.

'And I'm taking Ruby to her nan's for tea,' Ruby's mum said. 'That's why I was sort of hoping the library thing would go on much longer.'

'Mum!' Ruby says, and her mum giggles.

There's a photographer standing on the corner of Queen Street, and he snaps us.

'Great,' says Sam. 'Caught by the paparazzi on a wild Saturday night out with my little sister and her mates.'

'And me,' says Gracie, giving him a nudge.

'Listen,' says Jessi, 'whyn't you give that nice Prue girl a bell? Ask her round to eat with us?'

'Er. No,' says Sam.

'Now, Samuel,' says Jessi, 'from what I hear your future's back in place, so I don't see the reasoning behind staying broken up with your lovely girlfriend.'

'She's going travelling.'

'Not this summer she isn't.'

'Mind your business, Jessi.' He marches off.

Jessi winks at me. 'You should give her a call. Let her know what his plans are.'

Maybe, I think. Or maybe it will work itself out. Or maybe that doesn't happen. I still don't know.

We all say goodbye to each other, standing on the corner in a big cluster.

'See you tomorrow?' Ruby says.

'Yeah,' says Aiza.

'Yeah, definitely,' I say. 'Listen. You know.'

'We know,' says Ruby.

'I don't know,' says Aiza. 'What are you trying to say, Dallas?'

'Oh shut up.'

'No, go on, articulate it for me. Please.'

I push her in the face. She goes off with Sofia, laughing, and Ruby goes the other way with her mum to meet her nan, waving over her shoulder. Jessi puts her arm round me. She puts the other one round Gemma.

'What are you getting mushy for?' Gemma asks her. 'You aren't going anywhere.'

'Not yet,' Jessi says. 'Soon, though.'

'And you'll be coming back soon too.'

'Maybe.'

'Definitely.' Gemma pats her hand, awkwardly. 'You're always welcome.'

Jessi grins. 'Always? Because you know I'll probably take you up on that.'

Gemma has an expression on her face like she's seeing herself in a few months' time regretting this conversation. 'Oh, I know you will. You're a member of this family, aren't you?'

I leave them to their awkward moment and walk behind with Billy, holding his hand. He looks up at me. 'Am I a member of this family?'

'You?' I say. 'You're the memberest member we have. We couldn't do without you.'

'Why?' Violet twists round in front of us, hanging from Gemma's hand like a puppet. 'What's Billy done?'

'Nothing special. But we couldn't do without him. You neither. You don't have to do anything special for that,' I tell her.

She twists round again, then lets go of Gemma's hand and stops to take mine.

'We couldn't do without *you*!' Billy shrieks, prodding me in the stomach with his finger. And I hang on to both of them tight, because they probably could, if they had to. Do without me. But I'm super glad right now that they don't have to.

Acknowledgements

For this book particular thanks go to my lovingly forthright editors, Chloe Sackur and Eloise Wilson, who had a hand in its very dust. I also need to thank my agent, Robert Caskie, for all his help and advice.

When writing a book partly set in school, it's possibly an advantage to be working in one. I would like to thank the children of SS Philip & James' Primary School for their solid example, not to mention being among the first people to hear some of the story and to give their thoughts on its title. Some credit is also due to the staff, so I thank my colleagues there, and especially (of course) the Office dream team – you know who you are.

My friends and family have been as supportive and distracting as ever. All love to them, especially those who have selflessly been my companions on trips and holidays over the last while.

Mum, Dad – obviously.

Finally to those who put up with living with me – Oscar, Aobh, Jeff – you are the best people I know. And Pete, all the good stuff is down to you. Always.